MINOTAUR

SIMON CLUETT

Copyright © 2022 Simon Cluett

The right of Simon Cluett to be identified as the Author of the Work has been asserted by him in accordance with the Copyright, Designs and Patents Act 1988.

First published in 2022 by Bloodhound Books.

www.bloodhoundbooks.com

Print ISBN: 978-1-5040-8016-3

For Lisa
(My partner in crime)

TUESDAY, 21ST JUNE

9.27PM

He had been watching the family for weeks. Logging their routine in a spiral-bound notepad. Smudgy pencil sketches interspersed a jagged scrawl. His drawing of the husband depicted a handsome man with dark hair, prominent cheekbones and deep-set eyes. The boy was maybe six or seven, with a gap-toothed smile and a messy blond fringe. As for the wife's likeness, her almond-shaped eyes sparkled with warmth and there was a vibrancy to her shoulder-length hair. Viewed out of context, one might have assumed the artist nurtured an affection for his subjects. Perhaps even love.

Rain clattered against the hood of Minotaur's coat as he retrieved a holdall from the Subaru's back seat. Sucking in deep breaths of moisture-soaked air he strode across the leafy lane. A gnarled beech tree shielded the cottage. Only from the front gate was he afforded an unrestricted view. The property was illuminated by the buttermilk glow of a porch lamp. Rainwater pelted the long straw thatch. A stream gushed across ornate ridges, hammering the shingled pathway below, and speckling the geraniums with mud.

Minotaur tapped an eight-digit code into his smartphone and pressed Enter. An app cycled through a series of scans, tracking progress to zero in a matter of seconds.

Connecting... Overriding... Disabling... Success!

CHAPTER ONE

The TV show was loud and crude, but Zoe Knight didn't care. A glass of Shiraz was no longer an option, so reality shows had become her way of unwinding at night. She was stretched out on the sofa in a dressing gown and fluffy slippers. Strawberry-blonde hair lay in easy tangles around her shoulders. Her button nose had a light speckling of coppery freckles and jade-green eyes sparkled in the dim light. She caressed her swollen belly as silicone-enhanced divas launched into hysterics at yet another well-staged drama.

The pregnancy, although unplanned, had come at the right time. David's books were selling well, with each new release benefitting from an increased marketing budget. Even Charlie seemed fine with the prospect of a baby brother or sister. After their three-month scan Zoe and David had sat him down and explained the situation. Awkward questions were avoided with the lure of ice cream and waffles at Dickie's Diner. How Mummy came to have a little person growing in her tummy was left for another time.

Earlier that day Charlie had suffered an asthma attack prompting a frantic trip to A & E. The more he panicked, the worse the attack got. His inhaler usually took the edge off it but seeing him gasp for breath never failed to break Zoe's heart. As if that wasn't bad enough, the morning sickness showed no sign of abating.

Her day had begun at 6am. Lurching into the bathroom to spend several minutes throwing up. This raucous indignity was followed by waves of nausea and intermittent retching that lasted almost two hours. For now, at least, her metabolism had settled. With Charlie tucked up in bed she could finally relax. If David were home, he would be pottering around in her peripheral vision, making flippant comments about the trashy show. But he wasn't, which meant she could enjoy back-to-back episodes, free of distraction.

As if on cue, there was a knock at the door. Zoe groaned. It was probably one or even both, of the Merriweathers. If her elderly neighbours had ventured out on a night like this, it had to be serious. She sighed, struggling to get up from the sofa's loving embrace. "All right. I'm coming."

Reaching the front door, she checked the LCD wall monitor. Instead of a high-definition image of the person outside relayed from the smart doorbell, all she could see was a 'No Signal' message. Slotting the security chain into position, she opened the door.

The man outside wore a long coat with a hood that cast a shadow over his face. Rain hammered the waterproof material as droplets cascaded from the brim.

"Hello," she said. "Can I help you?"

He lifted his head and regarded her with the palest eyes she had ever seen. His features were eerily smooth. Possibly the result of alopecia, or chemotherapy. The unwavering scrutiny made Zoe feel like bacteria in a Petri dish. She was a half-second from closing the door when bolt cutters clamped down on the chain. Steel jaws sliced through brass links in a single snip. The man rammed his shoulder into the door with such force that Zoe was sent stumbling backwards. "Get out!" she shrieked. "Get out!"

She ran to the staircase, pursued by the clomp-clomp of fast-moving footsteps. Something struck the back of her head. White light filled her vision as she fell to the floor. In her last moments, before the claw hammer fell again, Zoe Knight thought of her unborn child... and little Charlie, fast asleep upstairs.

CHAPTER TWO

The publicity tour for *Rebel King* had reached Dublin. David Knight spent the afternoon at one of the city's largest bookstores. Having spent two years researching and writing his most ambitious novel to date, he relished the opportunity of getting out into the world again.

After an impassioned reading of the action-packed first chapter, David took part in a lively Q & A session, before signing copies of the book. His only other engagement that day was an interview with a reporter from *The Dublin Herald*.

They met in The Coin & Compass, a pub with authentic charm and a welcoming landlord. David warmed to the young journalist immediately. Niall Fallon had an engaging manner, and a hearty laugh that never felt forced or misplaced. Their conversation played out against a backdrop of folk music and the excitable pings and dings of a noisy fruit machine.

"So where do you get your ideas?"

David took a sip of Guinness and savoured the creamy bitterness. "History. The past is such a rich tapestry. Full of exciting and horrific tales. Assassinations. Conspiracies. Rebellions. That sort of thing is the perfect backdrop for a story, although I make it a rule never to change the facts. If it happened, that's how it plays out in my books. I look for the gaps and grey areas between what's known and what isn't. Speculation, confusion, and doubt – that's where mysteries and great drama can be found."

He could trace his passion for the subject back to Drummond Hill Primary School, circa 1978. He learnt about the Romans, the Egyptians and the Ancient Greeks from teachers who had first ignited, and then fanned the flames of his interest. During school holidays David spent much of his time at the local library. While his friends were out on their bikes, exploring and building dens, he would immerse himself in reference books about the Tudors, the Elizabethans, and the Victorians.

He went further and deeper throughout secondary school, sixth form and university. After graduating he somehow ended up in advertising, brainstorming pithy slogans for all manner of products. He was particularly good at writing copy for top-of-the-range cars and camper vans – ironic given that he had never passed his driving test.

He wrote his first novel, an epic thriller set during the American War of Independence, while on his daily commute. It sold well enough for David to hand in his notice and he never looked back.

"Can you give me a wee hint about what you're working on next?"

This was another frequently asked question, although the answer necessitated a delicate balancing act. His publisher would be less than happy if he revealed too much. On the other hand, it was important to whet his readers' appetite. "As a matter of fact, yes. What do you know about the Spanish Inquisition?"

"Only that no one expects it."

David smiled at what was a go-to response for most people. "Monty Python have a lot to answer for. It was actually a pretty nasty time."

"So, I'm guessing we can expect plenty of torture, suffering and death?"

"By the bucketload. I can't disappoint my readers, can I?"

"No, that wouldn't do at all."

Their conversation was interrupted by a chime from David's jacket pocket. He recognised it immediately as the tone he had assigned to Zoe's number. "I'm sorry, please excuse me. It's my wife."

David rang Zoe every day without fail. For her to call him was unusual as engagements often overran and she would end up with his voicemail. After hearing about Charlie's asthma attack and the trip to A & E, he was glad she had. Zoe tried to persuade him not to cut his trip short. By that point, Charlie was on a nebuliser and his breathing was back to normal. There was nothing David could do and by the time he was home, Charlie would be tucked up in bed anyway. David was having none of it. He explained the situation to Niall, apologised and promised him an exclusive on his next book. The two men shook hands and the jovial reporter insisted on giving David a lift to the airport.

David's flight back to England was fast, smooth, and uneventful. He had earmarked the time as an opportunity to start reading a reference book about Tomás de Torquemada. David set his phone to airplane mode and turned to chapter one.

The first Grand Inquisitor was a zealot. A Dominican monk whose fanaticism had driven him to commit countless atrocities in God's name. Hanging, burning, stretching, starvation and mutilation were all tools at his disposal.

Widely known as 'the hammer of heretics', his quest to purify the Catholic Church led him to torture and kill more than two thousand souls. He had played an horrific yet fascinating role in history and David was eager to weave him into the plot of his next book.

Face of the Assassin would feature a new protagonist. A French nobleman by day and a killer for hire by night. This would be the first in a series of historical adventures to play out across sixteenth century Europe. The central character, along with chunks of the plot, had occurred to David fully formed. It was rare but when it happened, he experienced 'the prickle'. Zoe had coined the term to describe the moment when inspiration struck and the hairs on the back of his neck stood to attention.

On more occasions than he cared to remember, David would write himself into a corner by placing his main character in what seemed like an impossible situation. It led to sleepless nights and thousands of wasted words exploring various escape options. The process was hugely frustrating – right up until the moment when the clouds parted, the sun shone through, and an exciting yet satisfying outcome was revealed. Like a junkie craving his next fix, he often found himself clamouring for that oh-so elusive prickle.

The plane touched down at a rain-lashed Stansted airport shortly after 8pm. All being well, and assuming no accidents or snarl-ups along the motorway, David would be home in a couple of hours. He popped into a duty-free shop to buy a bottle of Zoe's favourite perfume and an oversized chocolate bar for Charlie.

After negotiating passport control and reclaiming his suitcase from the baggage carousel, David made a beeline for the nearest available cab. Settling into the back seat he checked his messages. A slew of pings heralded the arrival of emails and text messages, but there was nothing more from Zoe. He tried to call her but there was no answer. At that time of night, he would have expected his wife to be watching TV, with her phone within easy reach. She must have gone to bed or dozed off on the sofa.

The rain was still hammering when the cab dropped David off at Oldcroft Lane. He hadn't packed an umbrella so was dripping wet by the time he slotted his key into the front door. "Hello? I'm home."

Peering into the living room, he was surprised to find an empty sofa and the TV in standby mode. He checked the kitchen, the utility room, and the downstairs bathroom. "Zoe? Your wonderful husband has returned from his travels."

David was about to head upstairs when his foot skidded on the floorboards, and he fell awkwardly. Wincing, he got to his feet but noticed a dark stain on the already damp fabric of his trouser leg. He stared at it for several long, terrible seconds before wiping his hand across the mahogany floor. No one could ever accuse David Knight of being a religious man but in that moment, he uttered a silent prayer.

Please God, don't let it be blood.

Primal instincts kicked into gear as he studied the crimson smudge.

"Zoe?" he yelled, bounding up the stairs. "Charlie?"

His palm smashed down on the landing light switch as he flung open the main bedroom door. The duvet was undisturbed, and colour-coordinated pillows were neatly stacked against the headboard. By the time David reached the bathroom his heart felt like it was about to explode. "Zoe?"

Instead of a gleaming white suite all he saw was red. The naked body slumped in the bath was female. One leg hung limply over the edge. Blood dripped from the toes to form a dark puddle on the tiled floor. David's hands trembled as they moved to cover a silent scream.

The more he looked at the ruined form the more features he

recognised. Sightless, jade-green eyes partially hidden by strands of matted strawberry-blonde hair. Zoe's breasts had been sliced away to expose the glistening meat within.

David vomited, sending a torrent of Guinness-tinged bile splashing through his fingers. He stumbled out of the bathroom, rebounding off the landing wall into the door of his son's bedroom. He shoved it open so hard the scuffed brass handle dented the wall.

Reaching for the light switch, David clung to the hope that his young son might still be asleep. The filament in the bulb flared, killing that fantasy in a heartbeat. The bed was empty. The *Toy Story* duvet thrown aside. A matching Buzz and Woody pillow lay on the floor. On the wall, daubed in blood as if drawn with a slow and deliberate fingertip, was a maze.

CHAPTER THREE

William and Iris Merriweather were playing gin rummy when they heard the sound. It could have been a howl of wind were it not for the hint of an actual word.

"Chaaar-lieee."

William laid his cards face down on the table and gave his wife a stern look. "No peeking."

"As if I would," said Iris, with a mischievous grin. After fifty years of marriage, they had experienced more than their share of good times and bad. But despite all the aches, pains and constant bickering, these two wily septuagenarians still adored each other.

William's bony fingers curled around his walking stick. He raised himself from his armchair and limped over to the window. Pulling back the flock curtain he peered outside. The porch lamp illuminated their rain-sodden driveway, but not much further than the front hedge.

"Chaaar-lieee."

"What's going on out there?"

Pushing his ruddy nose to the window, William could just

make out a vague figure in the road. "I reckon it's him from next door."

"Which next door?"

"You know... the writer."

"David?"

"That's the chap."

"Is he all right?"

"What am I, Mystic Meg?"

"Go and see what's wrong."

"Have you seen it out there? It's raining cats and dogs."

"You'd better take an umbrella then."

William mumbled to himself, playing the embittered curmudgeon. He let the curtain fall back into position and hobbled to the front door.

"Chaaar-lieee!"

The bedraggled man sunk to his knees as violent sobs wracked his body.

William approached cautiously, struggling against the wind to stop his umbrella from blowing inside out. Unlike his wife, who made a point of getting to know her neighbours, William had barely uttered more than the odd pleasantry to David. The sight of him now, apparently in the grip of a mental breakdown, made him uncomfortable. "Are you all right there, old chap?"

"Charlie..." David's voice was a whisper.

William knew this was the name of the Knights' young son. A reasonably well-behaved child who William often heard playing in the garden next door.

"What about him?"

"He's... gone."

"Gone? Gone where?"

David shook his head.

Spotting traces of what could only be vomit on his neighbour's shirt, William's mind raced to fill in the blanks. There had clearly been an argument. David's wife had stormed out and taken the boy, leaving David to drown his sorrows.

"Come on, old son," said William as kindly as he could manage. "Let's get you indoors."

CHAPTER FOUR

Frank Crocker had stayed with his daughter and grandson at A & E until the doctors gave the all-clear. He drove them back to their cottage and offered to stay the night – just in case – but Zoe was adamant that would not be necessary.

"Are you sure, love?" he said, in his usual gruff tone. "It's no trouble."

"Thanks, but we'll be fine. David will be home in a few hours."

Although in his sixties, Frank's time as a boxer had given him a bulky physique and an intimidating demeanour. His life had been a series of missteps and bad decisions but, thanks to Zoe and Charlie, it finally had meaning. He kissed the top of his daughter's head, just as he had on the day she was born.

After saying their goodbyes, Frank drove back to his bungalow. The day had taken a toll on him as well. He grabbed a beer from the fridge and strolled into the garden, barely noticing the rain, and stared at the infinite canvas above him.

The prospect of sleep seemed as far off as the Milky Way, so he headed for his workshop. Frank had bought the bungalow a year after his wife died. It was close enough to Zoe and David for childminding duties and ad hoc DIY jobs, but far enough away that there was no risk of being considered a nuisance.

Having lived in cities his whole life, moving to Little Dibden had taken some getting used to. The house itself was nothing special, but he was a man of simple tastes. He preferred a low-fi analogue existence to the digital trappings of this modern age. What had swung his decision was the extended double garage. When he moved in it was an empty space. Cut to five years later and there was barely room to move.

Frank paid the bills by refurbishing and selling household appliances. A workbench was fitted with a vice, a circular saw, and an angle grinder. Hanging from hooks across the plasterboard walls were an array of tools for every conceivable job.

He selected the smallest of his cordless screwdrivers to dismantle a tumble dryer and traced the problem to a faulty capacitor. As he rummaged around for a replacement, he heard the first siren scream past. The police car must have been going at least seventy miles an hour and it was closely followed by a second.

Little Dibden was as quaint as its name suggested. This was not an area troubled by soaring crime rates, or antisocial behaviour. To hear not one but two response vehicles tearing past was worrying to say the least. Especially given the direction they were heading.

Alarm bells ringing, Frank jumped into his pickup truck and set off in pursuit. Its headlights illuminated the narrow road that snaked through dense woodland towards Oldcroft Lane.

Frank's knuckles began to cramp from his vice-like grip of the steering wheel. He flexed each hand in turn, curling and uncurling his calloused fingers to get the circulation going. On the ring finger of his left hand was a chunky gold band. A permanent fixture since the day he and Lucy tied the knot. It had a comfortable weight that made him feel as if she was never far away.

A final bend in the road led away from the woods and into the village. Frank could just make out the duck pond on his left, moonlight glinting off the water's surface. On his right was The Three Keys pub, and the slowly crumbling tower of Saint Andrew's Church. He passed the tearoom and a shop that sold rare books and antiques. At the end of Oldcroft Lane were a cluster of thatched cottages where blue light flickered ominously in the wet night air.

Uniformed officers in reflective jackets were cordoning off the area. Frank's truck bumped up onto the pavement. He was drenched within seconds of leaving the vehicle.

PC Bennett, a young officer not long out of Hendon, looked up from the blue-and-white tape he was unreeling. He squinted past the waterfall streaming from the peak of his cap to see Frank striding towards him. "Sir? I must ask you to stay behind the line."

Frank ignored him. He ducked under the tape and headed for the cottage. Bennett sprinted across the road to block Frank's way. "Sir," he said, in his most authoritative manner. "Please stay behind the line!"

Frank bulldozed past the young constable. "Get out of my way."

PC Quinn and PC Munro hurried over. "Sir," called Quinn. "Go back behind the tape now or you'll leave me no option but to—"

"My daughter lives there."

The officers exchanged a sideways glance. Frank's granite-like features hardened further. "What's going on? Why are you here?"

"Sir," said Munro, "please—"

"I asked you a question: what's going on?"

"Frank?"

All eyes turned to David. He stood in the doorway of his cottage. A grey blanket draped around his shoulders. He clutched the fabric tight to his chest in a two-handed grip. He was ashen-faced, as if he had aged ten years in the last hour alone. Sergeant Coombes appeared at his side.

"David..." Frank's voice was a low rumble. "Where's Zoe? Where's Charlie?"

"They're..."

"What is it? David, talk to me."

"Sir," said Quinn, "come with me. You need to sit down." He attempted to loop an arm around Frank's broad shoulders but was batted away. Frank opened the gate and strode towards the cottage.

"I can't let you in," said Coombes. "This is a crime scene."

Frank took another step along the sodden path, but Munro and Bennett cut him off. Frank raised his fist, ready to take a swipe at anyone foolhardy enough to get in his way. Quinn grabbed Frank's wrist and spun him into an arm lock.

"That's enough!" yelled David. "Let him go!"

The moment Quinn released his grip Frank made a break for the doorway. The blanket fell away as David ran to him. He grabbed his father-in-law in an awkward bear hug. "I'm sorry, Frank. I'm so, so sorry."

"I have to see her!" Frank's voice cracked as his eyes glistened with tears.

"This is a crime scene," said Coombes, sounding like a stuck record. "We have to preserve the–"

"I want to see her!"

"No," David insisted, "you don't."

Frank blinked at the words, trying to comprehend their stark meaning. "Please... I want to see her. I want to see my little girl."

CHAPTER FIVE

I t wasn't long before the village's more inquisitive residents gathered at either end of Oldcroft Lane. Some at least had the pretence of taking their dogs for a walk, but others had no such excuse. They sheltered from the driving rain under their umbrellas, looking suitably concerned but hungry for gossip.

Three more squad cars and an ambulance arrived sending the rumour mill into overdrive. Officers went from house to house collecting statements while a search of the nearby woods and farmland was organised. A police helicopter hovered over the village until the downpour became a deluge.

Hopes had not been high from the outset. A large-scale search would have been a significant operation in good weather and during daylight hours. With the rain showing no sign of letting up, a decision was made at the highest level to postpone until first light. By then, the conditions were expected to improve.

In The Three Keys it was the only topic of conversation. Various outlandish theories were flying around. They ranged from a Jihadi terror attack to the discovery that Mr Nicolescu, a retired piano teacher, had been unmasked as a war criminal.

It wasn't long before the boozy regulars considered the possibility that Minotaur had visited their sleepy village. The tabloids had been covering his heinous crimes for the past two years. This brutal psychopath targeted Caucasian women, aged between thirty and forty-five. His third victim had earned him serial killer status, while victims four and five had brought him global notoriety. If Minotaur had indeed struck again, it would bring his body count to twelve.

David was only vaguely aware of paramedics, investigators and forensics specialists bustling around him. Their tone was courteous and professional, but he immediately

drew a blank on their names. "Find my boy. Bring him home." This frantic plea was his response to every question. He was taken to the nearby town of Carlton Bridge. Its police station was better equipped to deal with a major crime than Little Dibden's tiny Victorian equivalent.

David's fingerprints were taken, and his throat swabbed for a DNA sample. He swapped his blood-and-vomit-stained clothes for a grey tracksuit. His clothes and shoes were bagged, tagged, and admitted to evidence.

He was shown into a featureless interview room where he slumped into a stiff-backed chair. The mug of tea and the cheese sandwich he was given remained untouched. A police officer stood by the door, hands behind his back, staring at the opposite wall.

David followed his gaze but saw nothing of interest. His eyes tracked upwards towards the ceiling, past a hairline crack in the plaster, finally settling on a spider. It spun its web in the farthest corner of the room. David watched the creature dart back and forth as it constructed an intricate lattice. As the web took shape, the cloak of numbness began to lift, and David was overcome by emotion. The policeman glanced over but maintained a tactful silence.

David was still sobbing when the door opened, and a tall woman in her mid-forties entered. Her stern angular face was offset by a mass of frizzy red hair. She wore thick-rimmed glasses and a rust-brown corduroy trouser suit.

A well-groomed Asian man in his thirties followed her in. He wore an expensive suit and designer shoes but carried a box file and several folders that indicated he held a subordinate status.

"Mr Knight," said the female detective. "I'm sorry to have kept you waiting for so long. My name is Detective Inspector Maureen Rybak. This is my colleague, Detective Sergeant Vikram Prakesh." She paused, a look of compassion on her face. "Please accept my condolences."

She took a packet of tissues from her pocket, peeled away the plastic wrapping and slid them across the table. David took one and wiped the tears from his eyes.

"Have you found him?"

"'fraid not."

"Why are you here? Why aren't you out there, looking for him?"

"Please rest assured we're doing everything we can."

"This is him, isn't it?" spat David. "Minotaur."

"We're still piecing together the facts."

"Cut the shit. I saw the maze. It's his signature."

Rybak pursed her lips, as if mulling over how best to answer. "We tried to keep that from the press after the first murders. Alas, we failed."

She and Prakesh sat down on the opposite side of the table. The junior officer busied himself arranging the files neatly in front of him.

"We will find him," said Rybak, "you have my word."

"Your word? Well, that's put my mind at rest."

"You're angry. I understand."

"Did you see what he did to her?"

"Yes, Mr Knight. I did."

David turned to Prakesh. "Did you?"

Prakesh nodded, holding his gaze.

"So did I," said David, "and I'm a long way past angry."

"Can you tell us about your home security system?" Prakesh asked, breaking the uncomfortable silence. David's eyes widened. With everything that had happened he had not given it a moment's thought. Several exterior cameras were positioned around the cottage, including one that formed an intrinsic part of the doorbell. They were motion sensitive so would have been triggered by anyone approaching the property. "There'll be video of him," said David. "I have an app on my phone that controls it all. I was asked to hand it in."

Prakesh flipped the lid of the box file and removed a smartphone sealed in an evidence bag. "I have it here. Am I right in thinking your home is fitted with the Emperor 5 security system?"

David nodded. "It was installed a few months ago."

"And presumably the app on your phone sends a notification when a camera is activated. You then get an option to view the video stream."

David suddenly clicked where this line of questioning was headed. "I should have received an alert, but I didn't."

"Are you sure about that?"

"Positive. I checked my messages in the cab, on the way home. Why didn't I receive anything?"

"It seems," said Rybak, "the intruder knew how to disable your home internet remotely. No wi-fi means nothing would have pinged to your phone."

"And nothing would be saved to the cloud either," added Prakesh.

"But that shouldn't matter," said David. "It would be recorded on the hard drive. There'll be a video file on my computer."

"That's how the system should work, ordinarily."

"What do you mean, ordinarily?"

"Before leaving it seems the intruder restored your computer to its factory settings."

"Christ!" David spat the word out, his eyes burning with recrimination. "And what are you doing about it? Because it sounds to me like this maniac is running rings around you."

"We're pursuing various lines of inquiry."

"Such as?"

"Mr Knight–"

"Go on. Name one of these so-called lines of inquiry."

"I know this must be frustrating," said Rybak, "but I can't go into specifics."

"You don't have a clue, do you? I mean seriously, how long has this been going on? Eighteen months? Two years? You're not even close to catching him, are you?"

The detectives flinched as David slammed both fists on the table. "Stop wasting time. Get out there and find my son." He glared at them, shoulders heaving from the adrenaline surging through his body. Then his rage was hijacked by grief. He rocked back and forth, crying into clawed fingers.

Rybak went to comfort him. "Mr Knight, you have my word, we will do everything we can to find your son."

CHAPTER SIX

Minotaur maintained a steady seventy along the rain-lashed motorway. Windscreen wipers arced from side to side, squelching against the Subaru's toughened safety glass. The killer welcomed this bad weather. It kept people indoors, washed away evidence and generally hampered a police investigation.

This had been his most challenging period of surveillance to date – both physically and psychologically. So many hours spent hunkered down in the nettles and brambles across the road from the Knights' cottage. Shivering from the cold. Muscles screaming from the rigours of cramp. Gnats circling his dick as he pissed. But after enduring all that pain and discomfort, the stars had finally aligned.

He had learned of David Knight's travel plans by searching through the household rubbish. An unpleasant, but necessary, part of the process. Amongst the bean cans and lasagne trays had been a soggy itinerary for his upcoming book tour. The rain, coinciding with the trip to Dublin, had presented an ideal window of opportunity.

Minotaur signalled his intention to exit the motorway and

veered onto a slip road. The meeting place had not been his choice but having scouted the location beforehand he was satisfied the risks were minimal.

The old mill had once been a major employer in the area, processing grain and shipping flour to Europe and beyond. Production came to an inglorious halt back in the mid-nineties. Since then, the buildings and silos had fallen into disrepair. An attempt to develop the land was abandoned leaving it to become an urban graveyard. Daubed in graffiti and reclaimed by nature.

The Subaru pulled up alongside what had once been an administration building but was now a dilapidated shell. Torrents of rainwater gushed from broken guttering and somewhere, something metal creaked in the wind. Minotaur slid the key from the ignition and listened to the steady clatter of rain across the bodywork. He peeled back his hood to remove a GoPro harness. The nylon strap left a stippled imprint around his gleaming scalp.

Headlights flared in the rear-view mirror as a blue BMW rolled to a stop behind the Subaru. The door on the driver's side swung open and a hulking man with long grey hair and a beer gut emerged. In his shabby jeans, T-shirt, and battered leather Harrington, Peter Vaughan looked like a roadie for a three-chord rock band. He slid open a wide-brimmed red-and-white golfing umbrella before making a swivelling motion with his free hand.

Minotaur wound down his side window and felt the spatter of moisture on his face.

Vaughan's expression tightened when he saw the killer's eerily smooth features. "You're all over the news! What the fuck happened?"

Minotaur had not switched on the radio so was unaware of this development. The husband must have returned home earlier. Or maybe the father had paid his daughter an unexpected visit. "It's unfortunate."

"Unfortunate? I should have my fucking head examined doing business with you."

"If you walk away, that's your choice. I will, of course, expect full payment."

"And what if I say no?"

"That would be a mistake."

Vaughan chewed this over like a grazing heifer, then nodded. "Let's get this done."

"Yes," said Minotaur. "Let's."

He pulled a cloth from his jacket pocket and gave the steering wheel and dashboard a wipe down.

"I'll sort that out," said Vaughan, with growing impatience.

Minotaur ignored him. He turned his attention to the gearstick and glovebox, stopping only when he was satisfied that all trace of himself had been removed from the vehicle's interior. Using the cloth to open the door he stepped into the shelter of the tent-like umbrella.

Rain spattered the canopy as Minotaur thumbed a key fob to unlock the boot. He dragged out his tool bag and an insulated chiller box to reveal, in the cramped space behind, a child's bare foot. The five little piggies poked out from under a tartan blanket. Vaughan pulled the fabric aside and nodded appreciatively. "What did you give him?"

"Ketamine."

"How much?"

"Enough to knock him out for another couple of hours."

"Are you sure about that? I mean, it's not exactly been your night, has it?"

Minotaur forced a smile. This ignorant yob had outstayed his welcome. "I think that just leaves the small matter of my payment."

Vaughan tugged a bulging envelope from an inside pocket and passed it to the killer. "No need to count it. It's all there."

27

"When you move him, make sure you don't leave him lying on his back."

"Why not?"

"Because he could choke on his own vomit and die. I'm guessing you'll want to avoid that."

Vaughan didn't respond. Instead, he snorted phlegm from the back of his throat and spat into a puddle.

"Right then," said Minotaur. "He's all yours."

Vaughan dug out a car key and waved it at Minotaur. Instead of swapping it with his own, the killer stepped from beneath the umbrella to examine the BMW. Rain beat down as he moved around the vehicle. "What's this?" he asked, indicating a mound of duct tape holding the wing mirror on the driver's side in place.

"It's nothing. The previous owner had a ding."

Minotaur was struck by the sudden urge to stab this knuckle-dragging oaf in the neck with a screwdriver. "Change of plan. I'll stick with my car."

It was a risk, but so was driving away in a vehicle that had such an easily identifiable feature. Peter Vaughan could not be trusted to dispose of a soiled tissue, never mind a vehicle. But it did not matter. Minotaur had a contingency plan.

Vaughan lifted the BMW's boot as Minotaur scooped the unconscious tartan-swaddled child from the back of his car.

"Oh," said Minotaur when the boy was safely loaded. "I almost forgot." He pulled something from his pocket and tossed it to the big man. It arced through the air but caught Vaughan off guard and the catch was fumbled. The object hit a chunk of cinder block and landed in a puddle with a small plop.

"What's that?"

"The kid might need it."

Vaughan bent to retrieve an asthma inhaler from the puddle. Its cap was missing, and rainwater dribbled from the mouthpiece. "Ain't that sweet? Do you want me to read him a bedtime story as well?" But Minotaur was already back in his car and slipping the Subaru into reverse. Pocketing the inhaler, Vaughan watched him drive away.

A five-digit reward had been offered for information leading to the arrest and conviction of Minotaur. In some alternate reality, Vaughan would have alerted the authorities and staked his claim. In this reality however, the boy had a far greater value.

CHAPTER SEVEN

It wasn't long before tributes appeared by the front gate. Teddy bears, colourful drawings, and flowers – lots of flowers. From lavish arrangements to simple bouquets, hand-picked from gardens around the village. It was hardly surprising. Zoe had established herself as a popular and well-respected member of the community. She had a natural warmth and was a born organiser. Whether it was helping to arrange the summer fete, or fundraising events for the local primary school, she was always happy to pitch in and lend a hand.

Never one to take control, or push her own agenda, she was instead the voice of reason and diplomacy. When a local radio presenter was unable to switch on the Christmas lights one year, it was Zoe who came to the rescue. Even David was surprised to learn she had gone to the same college as a hunky celebrity chef. When David quizzed her about it later, she had been coy about the nature of their relationship.

David was one of the last to hear about the candlelight vigil. He went along with it, but only because it would have seemed churlish not to make an appearance. Joining the crowd, he took a candle and went through the motions. Seeing so many people he did not know, all holding their own little flame, was a surreal experience. Their grief seemed genuine enough, but it amounted to nothing when compared to his own.

When the vigil was finished, David walked back to Oldcroft Lane with the Merriweathers. His cottage remained an active crime scene, so Iris had insisted on taking him in. Their home was cosy, but the spare bedroom had a mustiness that a bowl of potpourri and a sprig of lavender did little to mask.

When David saw where he would be sleeping, he was immediately struck by how similar it was to Charlie's bedroom. The dimensions were identical. Swap the sun-faded floral wallpaper for a pale-blue matt, the antique wooden furnishings for modern, MDF equivalents, and the similarity was inescapable. Even the light fixture was in the same position.

David lay in bed, fighting the urge to scream, until 3am. Time had lost all meaning. The sun's position in the sky, the moon's orbit around the earth, the ebb and flow of the tides – none of these things mattered. His eyes stung from tiredness, but that mild discomfort was overshadowed by a rage born from impotence. But realistically, what could he do? The answer lay within easy reach on the bedside cabinet. He swallowed another of the pills Doctor O'Brien had prescribed before twisting the lid off a whisky bottle. David had never been much of a drinker. Combining alcohol with pills would not end well.

CHAPTER EIGHT

"**D**avid? It's time to wake up."

The voice was female but did not belong to Zoe. It was old, fragile and had a slight regional accent David was unable to place. Mumbling something unintelligible, he pulled the bed sheets over his head and tried to go back to sleep.

"David?" said the voice again. "That nice lady police detective just called. She said to tell you she's on her way so it's probably a good idea to get ready now. I've made you a nice cup of tea."

David forced his eyes open and saw Iris standing over him. She placed a steaming mug alongside the half-empty whisky bottle. Seeing it triggered three things in quick succession. First, an all-consuming sense of loss hit him like a sledgehammer. Then came a shooting pain, like a drill boring deep into his skull, courtesy of a savage hangover. Finally came the recollection that he was due to make a public appeal for information at a press conference.

"What can I get you for breakfast?"

"Nothing. I'm fine."

"You must eat something."

"I'm not hungry."

"I'll do you some toast and jam. Just don't go back to sleep."

She gave him a heartfelt smile before shuffling out of the room and closing the door. He reached for the tea but stopped before his hand was halfway to the bedside cabinet.

The bedside cabinet.

Why hadn't he thought of it before?

He threw back the sheets and thundered downstairs, ignoring the pain in his head. Iris was in the kitchen, buttering two golden brown slices of toast. "Are you all right, dear?"

David wrenched open the front door and raced outside.

———

PC Quinn stood at the front door of David Knight's cottage. He spotted the owner heading his way. "Can I help you, sir?"

"I need to go inside."

"I'm afraid that's not possible."

"I have to check something."

"Why don't you tell me what you need."

"I'll be one minute."

"I'm sorry. I can't let you in."

"This is my house."

"I understand that, sir, but I can't let you inside."

Quinn glanced over David's shoulder. Rybak and Prakesh had pulled into the driveway in their silver Audi. The detective inspector was first out of the vehicle. A mane of frizzy red hair billowed around her shoulders like Superman's cape.

"Mr Knight–?"

"Did you find his puffer?"

The question caught Rybak off guard. "I'm sorry?"

"The day it happened Charlie had an asthma attack. He was playing football with his friends. He got wheezy and started to panic. He has an inhaler. A couple of puffs and it opens his airways. Usually, he'd have it with him in his school bag but on that one occasion, he didn't. He'd left it at home. Zoe took him to A & E, and they were able to stabilise him."

"I'm sorry, Mr Knight," said Rybak, trying to keep up. "What are you asking?"

"His asthma inhaler. Did you find it?"

"It was probably collected as evidence. Where would it have been?"

"We always make sure it's in easy reach for him at night. Zoe would have put it on his bedside cabinet, next to the alarm clock. She would have read him a story and when he was asleep, she'd have gone downstairs. The puffer would have been on the bedside table."

"And you're sure it couldn't have been left anywhere else?"

"I just told you! They'd been to the hospital. Zoe would have made doubly sure it was there in case he woke up in the night and needed it. If it wasn't there, whoever took Charlie must have taken his inhaler as well."

Rybak turned to Prakesh, but the junior detective was already on his phone. He did not have to wait long for an answer. He thanked his contact and hung up.

"That was the evidence SRO. He's confirmed there's no record of an asthma inhaler. Not in Charlie's room or anywhere else in the house."

"Do you see?" said David, his voice almost manic. "Whoever took Charlie must want him alive."

"That's possible," Rybak conceded, "but let's not get ahead of ourselves. If Charlie is out there, then getting you in front of the cameras is even more important. Have you had a chance to draft a statement?"

"Yes!"

"May I see it?"

"It's up here," said David, tapping the side of his head.

"This isn't something you can go in and freestyle."

"I know what I want to say."

"Mr Knight," said Rybak, keeping her temper in check. "It's essential that you don't come across as judgemental or angry. The focus must be on Charlie."

She handed him a notepad and pen. "Draft what you want to say in the car, and we'll go through it in detail once we're there." She paused for a moment to look him up and down. "You're not planning to go like that, are you?"

"What's wrong?"

"It looks like you slept in your clothes."

"I did."

"Go and freshen up. We'll be in the car."

"This is a message to whoever has my son."

The emotion in David's voice was palpable as he addressed the reporters and camera crews. They had congregated in the assembly hall of Little Dibden's primary school. Rybak and Chief Superintendent Kenneth Ingles sat on either side of David. The walls around them were adorned with pictures Blue Class had painted following a trip to London Zoo. Charlie's picture was of a bright yellow lion with big eyes and lots of teeth.

"Charlie is seven. His birthday was last month, and he had a party with all his friends and family. Charlie is a wonderful, funny, and well-behaved little boy. He likes animals, drawing, football and playing with his toys. I love him so very much. He's my little star." David paused, struggling to maintain his composure. "If you have him, or you know where he is, please get in touch."

When David reached the end of his statement Ingles took over. The senior police officer's closing remarks covered the hotline details and were delivered in a typically professional manner.

Later, as cameramen gathered cables and packed away equipment, Rybak approached David. "You did well."

"I did what you told me to do."

"You humanised your son. At this stage, that's the only thing you can do."

"Humanise. It's an interesting word don't you think?" David's voice was heavy with subtext.

"The approach has yielded results in the past, but if you're looking for cast-iron guarantees, I have none to give."

"You said you'd find him. You promised me."

"Please be assured, we're doing everything we can."

"I hope so, Detective Inspector. I really do."

CHAPTER NINE

The painting was crooked. Not by much. Maybe as little as five degrees, but David noticed it immediately. His instinct was to straighten it but that would have meant leaning over the two middle-aged ladies sitting opposite him. He vaguely recognised them from around the village but with a gun to his head he could not have recalled their names.

It was a framed watercolour of Saint Andrew's Church, one of a dozen or so renderings of local landscapes that hung around the waiting room. They were pleasant enough but generic in style. Despite their modest price tags not one had been sold in the months since David had last visited the surgery. The recollection was all it took for his mask to crack. A simple memory of taking Charlie for a check-up had been triggered by a wonky painting.

David could feel the pitying looks from the two women. Like everyone else in the village, they would have seen his picture in the newspapers and watched his emotional appeal during the press conference.

Poor man.

How awful.

It's so sad.

David kept his eyes fixed on the carpet. The well-trodden flooring was dark red and had a delicate fleur-de-lis pattern. The stylised lily was an image often associated with European heraldry and French nobility. David had planned to reference the motif in his next book. The design had probably been a vivid gold when the carpet was first laid. Now, thanks to the constant footfall, it was a grubby yellow.

Doctor O'Brien appeared from her office, wearing her trademark tweed suit, and comfortable shoes. Fiona O'Brien had been Little Dibden's resident GP for decades. She was on first-name terms with everyone in the village and had known many of them since their school days or even birth. "David Knight?"

David glanced up and gave her a tight-lipped smile. He fought the urge to straighten the crooked picture on his way into her office.

"Please, take a seat," she said, settling back into her chair.

David sat opposite. His brow furrowed and his leg began to twitch.

"How are you coping, David?"

"If I didn't have the funeral to arrange, I'd be at home staring at the ceiling–" he paused, correcting himself, "–or rather, staring at the ceiling in my neighbours' spare room. To be completely honest with you, I'm struggling."

"Do you have anyone you can speak to about how you're feeling?"

"I have people queuing up to talk to me. I have my very own grief counsellor, a lady from the Victim Support Unit, several detectives, and a busload of reporters."

"I was thinking more about friends and family."

"Trust me, that's not the problem. I don't want to speak to people. I don't even want to be here, talking to you. No offence."

"None taken. So why are you here?"

David placed a small plastic pot on O'Brien's desk. It bore a printed label from the local pharmacy and contained three pills.

"Have you been experiencing any side effects?"

"Side effects? No. No side effects, but I may as well be sucking a mint for all the good they're doing. And before you ask, I've been taking them as you prescribed. One pill, three times a day. They're useless."

"It can be a few weeks before you experience noticeable improvement."

"There must be something else you can give me. Something stronger. Please." David waited for a response, growing uncomfortable from the doctor's scrutiny.

"Have they released Zoe's body yet?"

"Yes. Finally."

"And when's the funeral?"

"Next Wednesday."

"What time? I'd like to attend if that's all right."

"Of course. It's at eleven o'clock."

O'Brien turned to her computer and began typing. Her slow and deliberate technique suggested she would have preferred a good old-fashioned prescription pad to scribble on. "We'll try you on a course of Ventraxotine. You should notice a difference almost immediately. Take no more than two a day for the next seven days, but I want to see you again after the funeral. If you experience any nausea, drowsiness, or headaches you must come back immediately."

David thanked her and said goodbye. On his way out of the surgery he again had the feeling of being watched. This time it was a man in his mid-twenties. His long hair was tied back in a man bun. He wore cargo trousers and a black polo shirt with a yellow logo. Again, David vaguely recognised him but was unable to put a name to the face. He stared back until the man looked away.

The pharmacy was a five-minute stroll but David took a less obvious route to limit the risk of unwanted interactions.

"I don't have this in stock at the moment," said the chemist, returning to the counter. "I'll have to order it in."

Of course, thought David. *Why did I think it would be as simple as getting the thing I need, when I need it?*

"When can I collect it?"

"We usually get our deliveries around midday."

David nodded then turned away. He found himself looking down at an elderly lady hunched over a tartan shopping trolley. Her wispy hair had been lacquered into a pale-blue halo. "It's you, isn't it?"

"Yes. I guess it is."

"I saw you on the news. It's so sad. How are you, dear?"

Oh, I'm just dandy.

"Taking it one day at a time." It was David's stock response. A conversational Band-Aid for this sort of encounter.

"He'll burn in Hell for what he's done."

David was shocked by the venom in her voice. This old girl was not from the Tea and Sympathy brigade. It seemed she was strictly Old Testament. Her words echoed around his head as he made his way back to the Merriweathers' cottage.

In David's mind Hell was represented either by a little red devil brandishing a pitchfork, or the nine circles of torment envisioned in Dante's epic poem, *Inferno*.

If Minotaur was caught, it was likely he would be convicted and sentenced to life in prison with no possibility of parole. Maybe – just maybe – he would be stabbed to death by a fellow lifer. Or, given the extreme nature of his crimes, maybe he would be committed to the secure wing of a psychiatric hospital. Neither outcome was satisfactory.

In Dante's *Inferno*, murderers were condemned to the Seventh Circle of Hell, where they would drown in a river of boiling blood and fire for eternity. That, thought David, was more like it.

CHAPTER TEN

F rank was sprawled out on the sofa, unwashed and unshaven. He might have been mistaken for a corpse were it not for the raucous snoring. Waking with a jolt he blinked away the last remnants of sleep, his mouth stretching into a noisy yawn. With nails that were thick with grime he scratched the ragged salt-and-pepper beard that had grown unchecked. Anyone within a few feet would have recoiled from his body odour. Not that Frank would have cared. As far as he was concerned, time spent on personal hygiene was time he could have spent looking for Charlie.

Hauling himself up, he strolled over to a wall upon which an Ordnance Survey map of Little Dibden and the surrounding area had been taped. Certain quadrants were cross-hatched in green. Others in yellow. The location of Zoe and David's cottage was marked with a big red pin.

Emanating from this central point were a series of ever-widening circles outlined in blue marker pen. Each zone represented a quarter mile radius. Dotted across the map were Post-it notes covered in Frank's scrawl. Surrounding it all were headlines, articles and pictures torn from magazines and newspapers. They all shared a common theme – Minotaur.

Most concerned Zoe's murder, Charlie's disappearance, and the recent press conference. On the periphery were hundreds of column inches devoted to the previous victims and reports of police incompetence. The collage was annotated with dates and arranged in chronological order to create a rough timeline. It made for grim reading.

A total of thirteen souls had been snuffed out of existence. Twelve women, including Zoe, and Frank's unborn grandchild. The location of each murder was annotated by a black dot on a map of the British Isles.

Frank had read and reread everything a dozen times. Devouring every line of every clipping for some clue that might spark a light-bulb moment. But there was nothing. At least, nothing he could see.

Frank was operating way beyond his comfort zone. Maybe it was time for a new perspective. A fresh pair of eyes might spot the missing piece of the puzzle. Realistically there was only one person he could share this with. David was a smart fellow. If anyone could make sense of this sprawling tangle of information, it was him. But Frank knew what he would say.

Leave it to the police.

The chief superintendent had given both Frank and David his personal assurance that no stone would be left unturned. He had sounded convincing enough, and maybe he even believed it. Regardless, Frank's contempt for the police was borne from bitter experience. It would take more than a few platitudes from the top brass to convince him otherwise.

Frank retrieved a crumpled jumper from the floor and tugged it over his head, unaware of the ingrained stink. His boots were so caked in mud they were barely recognisable as footwear. Frank opened the front door and whacked them against the step, knocking off the worst of the dirt. As he knelt to tie his laces, he heard his knee crack and, not for the first time in recent weeks, a pain flared in his chest.

His first stop of the day was the library. He was greeted with a cheery hello from Barbara, who worked there part-time. Frank had become a regular visitor but although he kept to himself, there had been complaints about his dishevelled appearance. Barbara, however, knew what he had been through and thought it only right to cut the poor man some slack.

Frank headed to the photocopier. He unfolded a sheet of A4, slid it face down on the glass and lowered the cover into position. He jabbed in the number of copies required – two zero zero – before pressing a green button on the control panel. The machine whirred and swished as it churned out a batch of flyers. They spooled out of the side to create a neat pile in the first of three plastic trays. Frank was using a second-generation copy as a master, so the image quality was far from perfect. When the final sheet slid onto the top of the pile, he collected the still-warm copies and loaded them into a crinkled bag.

Frank left the library and went from door to door, pushing flyers through every letter box along his route. When he saw a parked car, he placed one under a windscreen wiper. Every so often he would tape them to lamp posts. It was an endeavour that took him the best part of the day. He then drove a mile out of the village, to a bumpy dirt track that cut through the westernmost edge of Little Dibden Woods.

The sun had dipped below the treetops and light was fading fast. Frank retrieved a torch from the back seat and followed the track. The flashlight's beam picked out a drop-handlebar bicycle that had been dumped in a ditch. Its frame was so bent out of shape it could only have been hit by a speeding vehicle. Judging by the advanced state of corrosion it had been there for years.

After almost an hour of searching he returned to the truck.

Flicking on the interior light he plucked a gatefold map from the cluttered dashboard and cross-hatched his location, the intriguingly named Witches Lane.

Frank had scraped together a thousand pounds to offer as a reward. It had prompted dozens of voicemail messages. There was no shortage of time-wasters and scumbags who were prepared to say anything to get their hands on the money. Frank soon became attuned to irrelevant, misleading, and contradictory information. Eventually one detail of particular interest emerged. Several callers had seen a black car on the night of Zoe's murder. Various makes and models were mentioned but they all agreed it was either black or dark blue and had been heading towards Carlton Bridge.

As he reversed along Witches Lane, Frank tried to think like the killer. Minotaur had consistently evaded capture which suggested he was no opportunistic madman. This was someone who took great care when selecting his victims and was adept at choosing the perfect moment to strike. Someone like that would not leave their escape to chance. They would know a downpour reduced the odds of their vehicle, and their registration plate, being spotted. They would also be anxious to get it off the road as quickly as possible. More than likely that meant swapping cars.

This had led Frank to begin a search of every lay-by, dirt track and patch of wasteland in a five-mile radius of the cottage. It was a bold ambition and there remained so much territory left to cover. Despite his naturally stubborn nature, Frank knew it was time to ask for help. He would speak to David about it at the funeral.

Slamming on the brake, Frank was suddenly struck by a flash of panic. Had he become so distracted that he had missed the funeral? He checked his watch. It was twenty-four carat gold, a present from Zoe for his sixtieth birthday. The inscription on the back read:

To the world's best dad. Love you forever, Zoe

The little aperture that tracked the date showed it was the 28th. Frank breathed a sigh of relief – the funeral was at 11am on the 29th, almost sixteen hours away.

He had planned to visit two other locations but had lost track of time. They would have to wait. He flicked the headlights on and continued reversing along the bumpy trail.

A single road snaked back to the village, so the route took him past houses he had leafleted earlier that day. If he had driven along Redmond Road five minutes earlier, or even five minutes later, there would have been no need for him to stop and get out.

A squat, bald man was walking along the pavement ripping flyers off lamp posts, balling them up and tossing them into the gutter. He had the squashed nose and flattened brow of a seasoned rugby player. Tribal tattoos curled around his neck and wrists.

"What are you doing?" called Frank.

"What's it look like? I'm getting rid of all this shit."

"That's my grandson. Put them back."

The man sneered and barged past. Frank grabbed his arm. It was enough to trigger an explosive right hook. Frank stepped aside leaving the impetus of the man's swing to propel him sideways. Pivoting on his left foot Frank kicked with his right. It struck the back of the man's leg with enough force that he buckled and dropped to one knee.

"This is me asking nicely. Put them back."

The tattooed man threw himself at Frank and they both went sprawling onto the pavement. A fist like a side of beef slammed into Frank's face and he tasted the coppery tang of his own blood. He could take one more punch like that, maybe two at a push, then it would be lights out for sure. It was time to fight dirty. Frank grabbed his attacker's windpipe, fingernails raking the epidermis as they dug deep. The tattooed man gagged and flushed purple.

"Let go! You're killing him."

Frank was only half aware of the newcomer's voice. A pair of hands grabbed his wrist and prised it away from the tattooed man's throat.

"Call the police," another voice yelled. "Now!"

CHAPTER ELEVEN

The Minotaur taskforce had taken over Carlton Bridge police station. Annual leave was cancelled and the pile of overtime claims awaiting approval continued to grow. Detective Chief Inspector Marcus Loveday prowled the incident room. Bulging muscles strained under his canary yellow shirt. With his shaved head, and neatly squared-off beard he had the look of a dapper mercenary.

It was 8.30am. Everyone across the floor stopped what they were doing to congregate around the ops board for morning prayers. Loveday held up the early edition of *The Sun* and gave it a contemptuous flick. The front page bore the headline: **Top Cop Flops.**

"I assume you've all seen this?"

There were weary nods and a chorus of mumbled yeses. Loveday scrunched up the tabloid and tossed it into the bin. "It's a kick in the nuts for sure but we can't get disheartened or distracted. We keep doing what we're doing until we get this bastard. He'll slip up. They always do. And when he does, we'll be there. In the meantime, if anyone is approached by the media, you know what to do."

Rybak wondered how many of her colleagues were suppressing the urge to suggest physical violence as an option.

Detective Chief Constable Lydia Peck had overseen the investigation since the beginning. Now she had been asked to step aside by the Home Secretary. This humiliating and all-too public indignity had followed months of escalating media criticism. *The Sun* had been especially vitriolic in what had become a crusade to get her off the case. It was as if she were personally accountable, not just for Minotaur's victims, but for every instance of violence against women.

Their efforts had finally paid off. Never mind all those years of dedicated service. Never mind the crimes she had been instrumental in solving. The murderers, rapists, paedophiles, and terrorists she had put away.

There were precious few serving officers in the upper echelons that Rybak could look at and say, 'Because of their courage, sense of duty and determination, this country is a safer place to live,' but Lydia Peck had been one such individual.

Zoe Knight's death, and the kidnapping of her young son, had compounded an already volatile situation. Now, the government had intervened, and Peck had been scapegoated. It left a bad taste in the mouths of everyone in the room.

Loveday took a hurried sip of coffee before seeking updates from his DIs. He listened to each summary before drilling into the detail. "Rybak, where are we with the Subaru?"

Rybak knew the question was coming. There had been multiple sightings of a black vehicle which several witnesses had described as a Subaru, or similar model. A partial registration number had been provided. 'E16', they had said. 'Definitely E16'.

"With just the make, model and a possible year of production to go on, all the DVLA can do is reduce a massive list down to a slightly less massive list."

"Anything from CCTV yet?"

"A few possibilities, but nothing definitive."

"What about scrapyards?"

"We've identified two front runners. Warrants have just come through. Vik and I are heading off straight after this."

"Keep me posted." Loveday turned to DI Yallop, a trim fellow with auburn hair and a mass of freckles. "What about lock-ups? Warehouses? Chop shops?"

Rybak could see Loveday was following up on everything any half-decent SIO should be doing. Nevertheless, she could not help but feel he was clinging on by his fingertips. Not that she could blame him. The case had become a meat grinder and Minotaur was cranking the handle.

CHAPTER TWELVE

Carlton Bridge Metal Recycling Ltd was a ten-minute drive away. Rybak introduced herself via the entry system, holding up her warrant card upon request. The towering metal gates slid aside with a low hum. Prakesh parked the Audi in a forecourt surrounded by stacks of wrecked and decommissioned vehicles. The detectives were followed in by a police van. Sitting in the back were eight uniformed officers, all eager to begin the search.

The site manager was an officious fellow who sported an elaborate comb-over and the hint of a moustache over his top lip. He ferreted around in the pockets of his hi-vis jacket, eventually producing a pair of wire-framed spectacles to examine the search warrant. Only when the document had been read in its entirety did his attitude change. He escorted the detectives into an air-conditioned office.

"We computerised our records about ten years ago after the taxman paid us a visit." He seemed to shudder at the memory. "It was the proverbial audit from Hell, but we took it as an opportunity to modernise our system and hire a bookkeeper."

Rybak didn't need a qualification in forensic accountancy to see their records were a masterclass in transparency and compliance.

Vaughan Scrap Metal & Car Spares was a different story. Spiralling razor wire crested a galvanised steel palisade fence which gave the premises a less than welcoming atmosphere. Lashed to the side of a demountable office was a tatty banner that flapped in the wind.

Cash payed for scrap!!! If its metal, We'll buy it!!!! 100% Garanteed!!!

The company clearly had a low benchmark when it came to their branding. The slogan also carried a whiff of desperation. Was this the sort of business that might consider making a vehicle disappear with no questions asked? Rybak's gut instinct screamed yes.

The yard was so littered with piles of scrap there was barely any room to park. The Audi just about slipped in between a skip filled with decaying engine parts and a pyramid of old tyres. The police constables waited patiently inside the van until the warrant was served.

As Rybak surveyed her surroundings she was struck by the acrid smell of engine oil. There didn't appear to be anyone around. The only sound was the chirrup of starlings perched on a gently swaying power line. Rybak's gaze fell upon the four-fingered claw of a grabber crane which hung idly over an ancient vehicle baler. Had those hydraulic jaws closed around the Subaru, biting into its bodywork, and shattering its windscreen? Had they hoisted the vehicle off the ground and swung it into the guts of the compactor? Had one hundred and fifty tons of force crushed the vehicle into an easily disposable cube of metal?

"What do you lot want?"

The voice was female and raw as if from years of smoking.

Rybak glanced around but saw nothing but smashed cars, corrugated iron, and dented oil drums. Elsewhere, the heavy doors of a freight container were ajar. She caught the orange glint of copper piping inside.

"My name is Detective Inspector Maureen Rybak. I would like to speak to the owner of these premises or the site manager." She glanced around, expecting a response that was not forthcoming. "This will be a lot easier if we can speak face to face."

A spindly woman with stringy curls and oil-streaked features appeared from under the rusting hulk of a camper van. She wore overalls and steel toe-capped boots. Her eyes shifted from Rybak to Prakesh. The young detective held the woman's glare, under no illusion as to what she was thinking. He had encountered that same look throughout his life, and it never got any more palatable.

"Are you the owner?" asked Rybak.

The woman folded her arms like a petulant child. "No."

"Okay, so who is the owner?"

"My Uncle Pete."

"Is that Peter Vaughan by any chance?"

The woman nodded.

"And you are?"

"Shelley Vaughan." She snorted, dredging something from the back of her throat and spat it out. A wad of phlegm hit the ground between her and the detectives.

"Is your uncle around? We'd like to speak to him."

"You're shit out of luck there, sweetheart. He's off on one of his golfing holidays."

"Where did he go?" Rybak let the 'sweetheart' comment slide, at least for the time being.

"I don't know. The Canaries probably. What's this about?"

"We have a court-authorised warrant," Prakesh said, sliding the document from his pocket. "It gives us the legal powers to search these premises. You are required, by law, to provide your full co-operation."

"Nope. Sorry. Didn't catch a word of that." Shelley turned to address Rybak. "What did he say?"

"I suggest you read the warrant," said Rybak, doing well not to slap the hate out of this dreadful woman. "You'll find it explains everything."

Shelley snatched the document from Prakesh's hand. Shelley's bony hands left grimy fingerprints along both edges of the fine-grain paper. She reached the end of the final paragraph, punctuating it with a muttered expletive. "Guess you'd better come with me then."

Rybak and Prakesh were led into the demountable office. It was as dingy and cramped on the inside as it was weather-worn and crumbling on the outside. As the door opened it knocked over a red-and-white golfing umbrella. It landed by a portable heater with a dust-choked grille. The plug was jammed into an already overloaded socket, from which a tangle of cables sprung. Power was supplied to a variety of office appliances including a computer, fax machine, and printer. Their plastic casings had yellowed with age.

Rybak indicated the ancient computer. "We'll need access to that."

"Too bad," said Shelley, slotting a cigarette between her puckered lips. "That thing's been on the fritz for years."

"In that case we'll need to look at your paper records."

Thumbing the wheel of her lighter Shelley touched the flame to the cigarette's tip. She took a long drag, savouring the nicotine rush and slumped down in a swivel chair. Several seconds ticked by before smoke was exhaled from the corner of her mouth.

Rybak could feel the last of her patience disintegrating. "I said–"

"I heard you! Jesus! What is it with you lot?"

She balanced her cigarette in an already overflowing ashtray before rummaging amongst an ecosystem of paperwork. From under a mound of bills she retrieved an accounting ledger. Its pages were dog-eared. The spine patched up with tape. Shelley made a point of reaching past Prakesh and handing the book to Rybak. Then she retrieved her cigarette, tapped away the ash and took another drag. Rybak locked eyes with her as she handed the ledger to Prakesh. It contained row after row of handwritten dates, descriptions, and a note of cash in and cash out.

"How long has your uncle been out of the country?"

"A few days."

"How many is a few days, exactly?"

"He went on Saturday. Today's Wednesday, right? You do the maths."

Prakesh indicated two entries in the previous month – the twenty-first and twenty-second of June.

"Were you closed on these days?"

"What's that?"

Prakesh turned the ledger around for Shelley to see. "There's nothing logged for either of these two dates. This was a Tuesday and Wednesday. Were you closed?"

"I'm sorry," said Shelley to Rybak. "I can't understand a word he says."

"Okay," snapped the senior detective, "all this – whatever *this* is – ends, right now. My colleague asked you a question. I suggest you answer him, or I'll arrest you for obstruction."

"Are you having a laugh?"

"No, Miss Vaughan. I assure you I am most certainly not having a laugh."

Shelley sucked on the cigarette as if a solution was hiding within its glowing embers. "Yeah," she said, eventually. "We were open."

"So, what happened? Why were those dates so slow compared to the rest of the month?"

"It's the recession. We have good days and bad days. Same as everyone else."

"Were you here on either of those days?"

Shelley exhaled, purposely clouding the air between her and the detectives. "Don't remember."

Prakesh stifled a cough and waved away the fumes.

"Right," said Rybak, reaching the end of her tether, "I think it would be better all round if we continue this at the station. Come on, *sweetheart*."

"What? No, wait—"

"Were you working on those days? Yes, or no?"

"Yes!"

"Good," said Rybak. "Now we're getting somewhere."

CHAPTER THIRTEEN

The sun arced across the sky and the uniforms widened their search. The whole place stank of fraud and dodgy dealings. There was a stack of evidence to pass on to HM Revenue & Customs, Trading Standards and the Health & Safety Executive but nothing pertinent to the Minotaur investigation. But it wasn't just the disappointment of another wasted day. That was bad enough but dealing with Shelley Vaughan had taken its toll.

Rybak was used to encountering the dregs of society. It was part of the job. Over the years she had been punched, kicked, spat at, and called all the names under the sun. On one occasion she had found herself staring down the twin barrels of a sawn-off shotgun. At least that experience, while terrifying at the time, had ended up with a big-name collar. Facing down toerags was so much more palatable when you ended up slapping the cuffs on them. As things stood, Peter Vaughan could expect a hefty fine or two, but it was not enough. Not when Prakesh had endured such a despicable level of prejudice.

They were sat at a table in Rybak's favourite haunt, Dickie's Diner. She had been a regular at this little café since transferring to the area almost six years earlier. Prakesh failed to see the appeal. The menu consisted of typical greasy spoon fare. A Jumbo this and an All Day that. His usual was therefore a glass of orange juice and a toasted teacake. The former had a thin acidic taste while the latter resembled something a child might have collected from a stony beach. He had discovered some wonderful eateries around Carlton Bridge but despite his best efforts they always ended up at Dickie's Diner.

"Are you all right?" said Rybak, midway through a bacon roll that was dripping with ketchup.

"I'm just gutted we didn't find anything. Shelley Vaughan's a delightful character, isn't she?"

"I can think of other words to describe that one. Listen Vik, you're a first-rate detective. You shouldn't have to deal with that kind of crap. Not from anyone, especially a poisonous little witch like her."

"Believe me, that was nothing. Besides, as my mum always used to tell me, every day before school, sticks and stones can break your bones but–"

"Words can never hurt you. Yes," said Rybak, gesturing vaguely at her untamed mass of ginger hair, "my dear old mum told me the same thing, but I get the feeling you probably had it worse than me."

"It's fine. Besides, it makes ignorant scrotes like her so much easier to spot."

He took a valiant mouthful of the teacake before admitting defeat and pushing it aside. Rybak was poised to take another bite of her bacon roll when she was interrupted by a melodic chime. Digging out her phone she called up the text message that had just arrived.

"Guv? What is it?"

"Frank Crocker has been arrested."

CHAPTER FOURTEEN

As her coffin was lowered into the ground, David expected Zoe to give his hand a comforting squeeze. That was Zoe all over. Regardless of the occasion she always knew what to do, what to say or when silence was the best and only response. She was at ease in all social gatherings, mingling and making small talk with friends and strangers alike. Keeping the conversation going while David struggled to recall names. She would be the first to hit the dance floor or pick up the karaoke mic. For anyone needing a confidante she would listen, advise, but never pass judgement.

Father Gull finished reciting the 'earth to earth, ashes to ashes, dust to dust' passage inspired by Genesis 3:19. The congregation watched as David scooped up a handful of dirt and scattered it onto the coffin. The ritual could be traced back to the days of ancient Egypt, with sand being placed on the body of the deceased before they were buried. David had the distinct feeling he was the only person to be thinking that.

When the service was over, David shook hands, hugged, and invited everyone to The Three Keys for drinks and a buffet. Father Gull, or Colin, as he encouraged parishioners to call him, waited for the crowd to disperse before making his approach. He guided David over to the oldest part of the church grounds. They stood amongst the lichen-speckled gravestones in the shadow of a sprawling oak tree.

"Thank you, Father. It was a lovely service."

"Now, David, I've told you before–"

"Colin, sorry. I hope you can join us at The Three Keys."

"Of course." The vicar paused, choosing his next words carefully. "I noticed Frank isn't here. I'm worried about him."

"You and me both. He didn't answer his door this morning and isn't returning my calls."

The vicar unfolded a sheet of paper and handed it to David. "I take it you know about these?"

David stared at the flyer. Printed on the crumpled A4 sheet was a grainy school photograph of Charlie. Handwritten, in marker pen, was an appeal for information, a phone number and mention of a reward. "Yes. I've seen them."

"He's going door to door, questioning people. I understand he's been quite abrupt, even rude, on more than one occasion."

"I've told him to leave it to the police, but he won't listen."

"Would you like me to speak to him?"

"It won't do any good."

"I know where Frank is liable to suggest I stick my prayers, but he needs to allow himself time to grieve."

"I'll check on him again later. See how he is."

The low beamed ceiling and horse brasses gave The Three Keys an olde-worlde charm. Its selection of cask ales and no-nonsense pub grub had brought it to the attention of CAMRA and made it a popular draw for visitors to Little Dibden. Today it was filled with Zoe's friends, relatives, and what seemed like half the village.

"It's a terrible business," said William Merriweather. His funeral suit swamped his frail body, but he had a spark in his eyes as he sipped a foamy pint of ale. "They should bring back the death penalty. Mind you, hanging's too good for that animal."

"William, please don't start. Not today," scolded Iris.

David excused himself to seek refuge in the gents' toilet. He opened the amber-tinted pot of pills and dry swallowed his second Ventraxotine of the day. The serotonin in his brain was raging and needed beating down. He closed his eyes and waited for the inhibitor to take effect. It was only when a velvety numbness swept over him that he returned to the bar.

The jukebox was pre-programmed to play Zoe's favourite songs. They jumped from decade to decade and genre to genre. Bubble-gum pop crashing up against grunge, goth, folk, punk and even a bit of good old-fashioned rock and roll. The mix was eclectic but there was no questioning her taste.

David finished his third double vodka and signalled to Glen the landlord for another. It was a long-standing joke that Glen found his customers to be a huge inconvenience. In a typically grudging manner he picked up a fresh glass and lumbered off in search of the appropriate optic.

David found himself surrounded by a group of Zoe's oldest friends. They were recounting funny and poignant misadventures from their university days. But while David gave the impression of listening, his thoughts were elsewhere.

'Hanging's too good for that animal.'

While everyone else had showered him with sympathy and gushing condolences, William Merriweather had nailed his colours to the wall.

Blunt force trauma to the head had been the official cause of death. The full post-mortem report had yet to be released but there would be nothing in the coroner's findings that David did not know already. He had seen the extent of Zoe's injuries with his own eyes. Her wounds were burnt into his retinas and would haunt him for the rest of his life. William was right. Hanging was too good for this animal.

David knew that if the procedure was carried out correctly the neck is broken, and death is instant. However, if the noose is tied incorrectly, muscles in the neck and along the spine are torn. The victim jerks and spasms – a movement known as the Hangman's Jig. Death from asphyxiation could take up to five or six minutes. Although preferable, it was still far from sufficient. More effective, thought David, was the gibbet. He knew a thing or two about the device, having researched it for one of his books.

As the conversation around him turned to Zoe's rowdy hen night, David imagined a world in which Minotaur was imprisoned in a body-shaped iron cage and suspended from a gallows-like structure. The bastard would die of thirst, hunger, or exposure, whichever came first. Although an effective deterrent, the stench of decay had led to the practice being discontinued as a risk to public health.

When Glen returned with the double vodka David knocked it back in one.

"Mr Knight? I'm sorry to interrupt."

Rybak's voice popped David's macabre bubble. He tried to focus but was feeling woozy. The detective stooped to avoid hitting her head on the low ceiling beams. "Can I have a word please?"

"Have you found my son?"

"No, but I need to speak to you. Alone, preferably."

"Let me guess, you're here to offer me your condolences. Well, you know what? You can stick your condolences. Get out there and find my boy!" David's voice had sufficient edge and volume that everyone in his immediate vicinity could hear his outburst. Zoe's friends, Glen the landlord, Doctor O'Brien, Father Colin, and the Merriweathers, all turned to watch in stunned silence.

"Mr Knight," said Rybak, her expression stoic, "this is about your father-in-law."

CHAPTER FIFTEEN

David's third Ventraxotine required a few dry gulps to swallow but it did nothing to repel the waves of nausea. He was in a cab, speeding towards Carlton Bridge police station. Rybak had tried to convince him not to make the journey. Frank was still 'helping with enquiries' and visitors would not be allowed. If David chose to ignore this advice, he would be turned away for sure.

Resting his still-spinning head against the cool glass he watched the woods flash by. Was Charlie's body out there somewhere, waiting to be found by some unsuspecting dog walker? Had he been drugged, or asphyxiated while he slept? His limp body scooped up and carried out? If Charlie had been strangled or smothered, then why take the unnecessary risk of removing his body, only to dump it a short distance away?

If that were the case, why take the inhaler?

David knew what a sick world his son had been born into. Every day the news was full of stories about people trafficking and paedophile rings. Considering the alternatives, maybe it would have been kinder if Charlie had been killed in his sleep.

The cab dropped David outside the police station. He paid

the fare and staggered into the building. "You've had my father-in-law locked up since last night. His name's Frank Crocker. I want to see him. Now!"

The duty sergeant was a thickset fellow with an impressive head of lambs-wool hair. "I'm sorry but that isn't possible. Your best bet is to go home, sleep it off, and give us a call tomorrow morning. I'll call you a cab if you..." His voice trailed away at the sight of David's face. David had gone from drunken bullishness to looking as if he were about to throw up.

"Where's the...?" His words were accompanied by the sting of bile in his throat.

The police officer jabbed a stubby thumb in the direction of the gents. "Through those double doors then first on your left."

David made it with seconds to spare. He slammed the cubicle lock into position, wrenched up the toilet seat and vomited. A foul-smelling torrent splashed into the bowl. He had not eaten, so what he brought up was mostly liquid. He heaved until there was nothing left, then wiped the seat and flushed. Emerging a few moments later he washed his hands and splashed cold water across his face.

He was poised to swallow another Ventraxotine when he caught his reflection and froze. Zoe was behind him, slowly shaking her head. David spun round, hoping to hold and kiss her one last time. There was, of course, no one there but for a moment he was sure he could smell her perfume. Sweet and floral but not overpowering.

The duty sergeant watched as David tried to maintain focus while veering back towards the front desk. "Do you want some water?"

David managed a nod as he took a seat in the waiting area.

The last time he had visited Carlton Bridge police station was the night of Zoe's murder. In the intervening weeks he had barely given it a moment's thought. Sitting there, in a funeral suit covered in flecks of his own vomit, he recalled that first interview.

Rybak had promised she would find Charlie. During their subsequent conversations she had revealed nothing about the investigation. He had no idea who had been interviewed or what leads were being followed up. It seemed the police were no closer to finding Charlie or tracking down the killer. David had naively assumed Rybak's eccentric appearance masked a formidable crime-solving intellect. With her wild hair and ridiculous dress sense she was no more than a platitude-spouting circus clown. She had failed to appreciate the significance of Charlie's missing inhaler. What other clues or vital evidence had been overlooked?

"Here you go," said the duty sergeant, returning with a bottle of mineral water.

David took a long and refreshing gulp.

"The other fella's out of hospital," said the duty sergeant, "but he seems hell bent on pressing charges. Look, I'll let Mr Crocker know you were here but there's nothing you can do for him right now. Let me call you a cab." He gave David a pat on the shoulder before returning to the front desk.

As David took another glug of water he glanced around at the anti-drugs and social awareness posters that adorned the grey walls. They issued stark warnings on knife crime, bike theft, drink-driving, and substance abuse. It was as if he were seeing them for the first time.

So much of his last visit remained a blur but his return had stirred a memory. Rybak's subordinate – the handsome Asian detective – had asked a question that now loomed large in David's mind. *'Can you tell us about your home security system?'*

The hairs on the back of David's neck tingled. A prickle that came from nowhere, but not because of some well-crafted plot twist. This time it meant he was in touching distance of remembering something important. The sensation was like being reacquainted with an old friend.

Ever since that terrible night David had been wallowing in despondency. Reliant on antidepressants and the contents of a bottle to get him through the day. None of those things would help to find Charlie. He had revealed himself to be as useless as Rybak.

"Five minutes."

David threw the duty sergeant a quizzical glance.

"The cab," the police officer clarified. "It'll be five minutes."

David barely registered the words.

The security system. What about it? Think!

The killer's arrival should have been recorded. That did not happen because David's wi-fi had been disabled and his computer's hard drive wiped. The prickle was showing no sign of relenting. If anything, it was getting stronger. David was zeroing in on something – but what? The system perhaps? According to Zoe it had been well reviewed, yet clearly there was a flaw.

And what about the installation process? Had something out of the ordinary occurred? Was this more to do with the security company, or the engineer? Zoe had arranged two or three quotes. She had outlined the pros and cons which had led them to decide who would get their business. But no, that wasn't quite right. There had been a discussion, and a decision made, but another company had ended up getting the job.

David cursed himself for always being so wrapped up in his own thoughts. As Zoe chatted about her day, or issues arising from the school newsletter, David tended to drift off and think about plot points and character arcs. He would nod or shake his head as appropriate, offering an odd word here and there to give the pretence of engagement. He usually got the gist but so much detail would be missed along the way. Had there been a cold call? Had Zoe been charmed by a persuasive sales rep? Or had another company's price been too competitive to resist? Either way, was it possible she had been manipulated?

"Mr Knight? Your cab's outside."

David didn't hear. His mind was racing. Mentally assembling jigsaw pieces without the benefit of any straight edges or even a picture on the box.

"Mr Knight, did you hear me?"

The engineer had installed the security system while David was in the house. After a solid four hours researching Torquemada, he had strolled downstairs to make a sandwich. The man he found in his kitchen, screwdriver in hand, was in his mid-twenties. He had long, greasy hair, tied back in a man bun.

"I said your cab's waiting outside."

"Give me a minute, will you?"

The policeman's bushy eyebrows knitted together, unimpressed by David's curt response.

A man in his mid-twenties. Long, greasy hair. Tied back in a man bun.

The engineer might have introduced himself but if he had, David could not recall his name. Nevertheless, he was certain of one thing. That same man had been sitting in the waiting room of Doctor O'Brien's surgery and had stared directly at David. Of course, David's face had been all over the news. Everywhere he went, people gawped at him as if he were some malformed wretch in a Victorian freak show.

"Come on," said the duty sergeant. "Let me help you up." He strolled over and offered David his hand.

"I'm fine right here."

"That's not an option. Come on, it's time to go home."

"I want you to get whoever's in charge down here right now. I need to speak to them. I have important infor..." The word withered and died in his mouth. "No... wait," he said, performing the verbal equivalent of a U-turn. "Thanks. You've been very kind."

David hurried from the police station and clambered into the waiting cab. He gave his address and was back at Oldcroft Lane in good time.

There was no longer an officer posted outside his cottage although blue-and-white tape still criss-crossed the front door. No one had told him he could not move back in – at least, not explicitly – so he entered the cottage for the first time in what felt like a thousand years. Without the Ventraxotine in his system he could feel tremors of emotion that would shortly become an avalanche. With tears prickling his eyes, he fought the urge to curl up on the floor and pray for death.

That's enough, he chided himself. *No more self-pitying bullshit!*

As he walked along the gloomy hallway, he could tell the place had been searched. The telephone table was askew. A framed photograph on the windowsill was in the wrong position. A picture of Zoe and Charlie on a beach in Jamaica. They looked so happy on the white sand. A sapphire-blue sea sparkling in the background.

David headed upstairs to his office and pulled open the top drawer of a filing cabinet. He retrieved a plastic wallet containing the Emperor 5 instruction manual, warranties, an invoice from Trinity Home Security Services Ltd and a business card. There was a name printed in a 12-point Helvetica font.

Ellis Jenrick.

David pocketed the card and placed the folder back in the drawer. There was one last thing to do before leaving the cottage. He opened Charlie's bedroom door and, for a moment, saw himself reading to his son. The little boy's eyelids were heavy, a minute or so from nodding off. The phantom image dissolved, and David was alone again. His eyes flicked to an image on the wall. A maze, drawn by the killer in Zoe's blood.

Charlie's collection of arts and craft supplies were neatly packed away in a storage box. Paints, crayons, felt-tip pens, stickers, glue, and a stack of coloured card. David grabbed what he needed and began to draw.

CHAPTER SIXTEEN

The fabric on the arm of the chair had been almost entirely picked away. A few loose strands were surrounded by a wasteland of threadbare material. Chunks had been excavated from the padding beneath to form spongy craters. The chair did not offer the best angle on the television, nor did it offer the incumbent a view of the grounds. It was not even particularly comfortable. None of that mattered to Alice. As far as she was concerned, it was her chair.

On several occasions she had experienced a meltdown upon finding someone else sitting there. As experienced as the care workers at Greenacres were, nothing they did or said had any effect. The only way of getting Alice to calm down was to let her sit in her ragged chair. In all other respects, she was a model resident.

Christopher Wynn weaved his way through the day room, towards Alice. Now that his hair and especially his eyebrows and lashes had grown back, he was unrecognisable as his monstrous alter ego – Minotaur. "Hi Mum," he said, kissing Alice's cheek.

"Who are you?" The old lady's voice was barely audible.

"It's me. Your son."

"Oh..."

They were joined by Kim, a care assistant in her early forties. She had luminous eyes and a cheery smile. Her dark hair was tied back in a neat braid. Despite the simple design of her tunic, its material clung fetchingly to her curves. "Hello again. I haven't seen you for a while."

"I know." Wynn did a good job of sounding contrite. "I feel terrible, but I have to be away from time to time because of my job."

"What do you do?"

"I put on exhibitions."

"Really? What sort?"

"Art installations mainly."

"That sounds so interesting."

"It has its moments."

"Well, you're here now and that's what matters. Can I get you a cup of tea?"

"Yes please."

"It's milk and two sugars, isn't it?"

"You remembered. I'm impressed."

"Don't be. As superpowers go it's pretty lame."

Wynn flashed what he called his genuine smile, designed as it was to reach his eyes and convey warmth, rather than to simply reveal his front teeth.

"And what about you, my dear?" Kim leant down to Alice's eye level. "Would you like a nice cuppa and some biscuits?"

"That would be lovely," said Wynn. "Thank you."

Kim made an 'aww' face and bustled off to make the drinks.

When all conversational merit had been wrung from the news and weather, Wynn moved on to the more mundane aspects of his own life. Minor repair jobs he had carried out around the house and which flowers were blooming in the garden. Alice was oblivious. Adrift in a world she no longer recognised or understood. Her reality was a patchwork of fading memories that lacked chronology and context.

"Here we are," said Kim, setting a tray loaded with tea and a selection of biscuits on a nearby table. She handed one steaming cup to Wynn then knelt to address Alice. "I made it nice and milky, just how you like it."

The sky was a kaleidoscope of orange and magenta by the time Wynn left Greenacres. He took several deep breaths as he strolled across the car park. There was only so much of the heady cocktail of cleaning products, air freshener and disinfectant he could take.

"Are you all right?"

Kim had changed out of her uniform into leggings, trainers, and a loose-fitting hoodie. A neon yellow helmet was perched on her head, and she carried a lightweight fold-up bicycle.

"I'm fine," said Wynn. "It's just... "

"I know. It can be intense at times." Kim pressed a button to release the bike's wheels and manoeuvred its frame into position with well-practised ease. "She likes you visiting."

"How can you tell?"

Kim shrugged. "I don't know, but isn't it better to think she does?"

Instead of responding Wynn stared into her eyes. They were hazel with green flecks. A well-judged flick of mascara had been applied to the lashes.

"What?" she asked, as if suddenly feeling self-conscious. "Have I grown a second head or something?"

"No, of course not. I think you're very pretty."

Kim's cheeks flushed red. She appeared to be lost for words.

"I'm sorry. That was completely inappropriate."

"No," said Kim, her cheeks still showing signs of colour. "I mean..."

"I should go." Wynn backed away towards his car. "See you next time maybe."

Wynn thumbed his car key. The alarm of a nearby vehicle deactivated with a modest blip-blip. He settled into the driver's seat, still feeling her watching him. Surveillance of the Knights' cottage had been a feat of endurance. His swansong, by comparison, would be so much simpler.

CHAPTER SEVENTEEN

Rybak and Loveday watched Frank's interview on a monitor in the room next door. His answers were mostly of the yes or no variety, prompting follow-up questions from a detective who was running low on patience. Frank looked older than Rybak remembered, and he had a faraway look in his eyes.

"So," said Loveday, "was he on your radar?"

"No. This took us all by surprise. But it sounds like he was provoked."

"You've read his file. You know what he did."

"That was a long time ago. People change."

"I don't care if he's been volunteering in a Romanian orphanage for the last twenty years. Frank Crocker is a vicious bastard. Keep an eye on him."

Despite the best endeavours of his solicitor, Frank was charged with assault and released from custody pending a date for the hearing. David collected his father-in-law, and they took a cab home. Frank was silent throughout the journey.

"Where's your key?" David asked when they were standing at Frank's front door.

Frank looked at him blankly, appearing not to register his surroundings.

"Your key. Do you have it on you? Is it in your coat?"

Frank patted himself down, as if he were a stranger in his own clothes. Eventually he produced a fob which David plucked from his hand. Opening the front door he flicked on the hall light, and guided Frank inside. Some post lay on the mat. Mostly bills and junk mail.

"Get yourself to bed. I'll fix you something to eat."

Frank nodded vaguely and did as he was told. For as long as David had known him, his father-in-law had never shown a hint of vulnerability. Had Zoe ever seen this side of him? Probably not.

The kitchen cupboards were well-stocked with tinned goods and there were plenty of frozen supplies. Fresh food was a different story. Apples were rotten, bread was stale and there was half a pint of lumpy milk in the fridge. The only plates and cutlery Frank owned were piled in the sink, congealing in a greasy soup.

David rolled up his sleeves and blitzed what he needed. He had already planned to stay the night, regardless of whether an invitation was forthcoming. Frank was family. Their shared grief should have brought them together. Instead, they had gone off in separate directions. David would not make that mistake again.

He prepared a banquet of chips, beans, and little pork sausages, delivering it to Frank's bedroom on a tray with a mug of watery cocoa. The snoring told him he need not have bothered. His father-in-law was sprawled out on the bed, still fully clothed. David set down the tray and, as quietly as he could manage, pulled a blanket over the slumbering form.

He finished the washing-up, made a hot drink and headed for the living room. Where he had expected to see a bookshelf and a collection of family photos, was an Ordnance Survey map surrounded by newspaper cuttings and handwritten notes. Brow furrowing, David studied the collage.

His brain scrambled to make sense of what he was seeing. He set down the mug, hooked his reading glasses into place, and moved in for a closer look. He read everything. Some things more than once. The commitment, the level of detail, the search Frank had single-handedly carried out was, in a word, remarkable.

"Frank? Wake up."

David gave his father-in-law a gentle shake. Frank half snored, half grunted. David gave him another shake, this time harder. "Frank? I need you to wake up."

Still no response.

"It's about Zoe."

His approach was harsh, cruel even, but it had the desired effect.

"What?" Frank murmured, rubbing his eyes.

"Come with me."

Frank dragged himself out of bed and followed David into the living room.

David indicated the wall. "You pieced all this together yourself?"

Frank yawned and nodded.

"Why didn't you tell me?"

"Tell you what? It's a bunch of dead ends. I'm not one step further than when I started."

"Look at it! You've established a timeline, you've ruled out leads. You've even got the bastard's car."

"A black car with no registration number. A fat lot of good that is to anyone."

"What if we can link it to a suspect?"

"How do you suggest we do that?"

David pulled out the business card and Frank gave it a cursory glance. "Who's Ellis Jenrick?"

When David had finished explaining, Frank slumped onto the sofa. "What's your point?"

"My point is that between us, we might know more than the police."

Frank had never had a good word to say about the cops, but only now could David see their ineptitude for himself. "We can't trust them to find Charlie. It's got to be us."

Frank's eyes narrowed to slits as he appraised David. "Before you go any further there's something I need to tell you. I had a run-in with the law a while back. I did ten years for armed robbery."

David's mouth formed a perfect circle. His father-in-law might just as well have said he had discovered a cure for cancer.

"It was a gold bullion job. I'm not proud of it but that's what happened. I was caught, and I did my time."

"Did Zoe know?"

"It was before she was born. If she suspected something she never asked about it."

"So, this assault charge... it's not a first offence."

Frank shook his head. "According to my brief, that's a problem. The bottom line is, if someone hadn't dragged us apart, I could have killed him. So, if you're asking me to have a little chat with this Ellis Jenrick character, and it turns out he knows something, there's only one way that will end. I'm fine with that. The question is David, are you?"

CHAPTER EIGHTEEN

Frank watched a long-haul lorry pull out of the depot. It carried a freight container bound for the continent. He had showered, shaved, and changed into what, for him at least, were fresh clothes. His jeans and cable-knit jumper were not smart or new, but at least they were clean. He stood by a sleek desk in the newly built administration block. It was a position that afforded him a panoramic view of the sprawling site.

"Quite something, isn't it?"

A petite woman with piercing blue eyes and bobbed, raven-black hair entered the room. She wore a striking white trouser suit and a pair of killer heels. Her aura stated, loud and clear, 'underestimate me at your peril'. "It's good to see you again, Frank."

"Natasha!" A rare smile broke across Frank's weathered face. They shared a warm embrace, genuinely pleased to see each other.

"I heard what happened. I'm so sorry. Are the police any closer to finding Charlie?"

Frank shook his head, eyes downcast.

"Dad asked me to pass on his condolences."

"That means a lot. How is he?"

"Not good. The doctors say he has six months. Maybe a year."

Frank said nothing, but his silence spoke volumes. He and Eddie Grand went back a long way. There was a lot of history between them. Some of it good.

Natasha smiled, taking a moment to wrangle her own emotions. "If there's anything you need, just say the word. The family are here for you."

"There is something."

"Name it."

"Close the door."

The gravity of his tone caused Natasha's expression to harden. Her stare was so intense it had earned her the nickname Laser-Beam Eyes within the company. Not that any of her employees would have had the balls to say it to her face. She closed the door while maintaining eye contact.

"What's this about?"

"I need a gun."

Natasha nodded, biding her time before answering. She was not thrown by the request, nor did she doubt Frank's ability to pull the trigger. "If you'd come to me a few years ago then I probably could have arranged something. But what you see out there is a hundred thousand square feet of commercial real estate.

"I have a fleet of eighty vehicles. We're talking millions of pounds of investment. Do you know what it's been like, dragging my family name out of the gutter and turning this business into a legitimate concern?"

"I'm sorry. I didn't mean to put you on the spot."

"Frank, come on... You've done so much for my dad – my whole family for that matter. You've earned the right to ask a favour. But guns... I'm sorry... that just isn't part of the world I'm in anymore. And for what it's worth, I think you should let the police handle this."

"I appreciate your time. I'll see myself out."

"Don't rush off. Come on, let me take you to lunch. I know this lovely little Chinese restaurant. Their Singapore spicy chicken is out of this world. What do you say?"

"Another time maybe. Congratulations by the way. What you've done here is incredible. You should be proud of yourself."

"I am, but this isn't about me, is it?"

"No, but it's not your problem either."

"Frank–"

"Goodbye, Natasha."

Frank sat in his truck for several minutes, hands resting on the wheel but making no move to start the engine. He looked past a diagonal slash of bird shit on the windscreen to focus on the back end of an eighteen wheeler. It bore The Grand Haulage Company logo, a less than imaginative arrow circumnavigating a wire frame globe. Underneath were the words, *Any load, Anywhere.* That could have been Frank's job description back when he worked for Eddie Grand. The only difference, it seemed, was the contents of these lorries were now kosher.

Frank had known that asking Natasha for help would be a long shot. Her response meant he would have to improvise.

CHAPTER NINETEEN

W ynn checked his watch – it was 8.10am. Kim usually left her flat at eight on the dot. Greenacres was a twenty minute bike ride away, and that was with a fair wind and little to no traffic. She would have to pedal as if chased by the hounds of Hell if she were to clock in on time.

Another minute ticked by. Then another. Finally, the front door opened and there she was. Her hair hung in soggy clumps around her face. Wynn didn't know if she had overslept or been delayed by some domestic crisis. Either way, she looked flustered as she lugged her bike down the front steps. The unfolding process took more effort than usual, and it was another few minutes before she set off.

Wynn was far enough along the road that he would not be spotted. At least, not by her. Anyone out for an early morning stroll might notice him loitering amongst the row of beech trees. Casting a furtive look around, he swung a rucksack over his shoulder and made a beeline for her flat.

What had once been a three-bedroom house had been converted into two one-bedroom apartments. A Yale lock clicked, and the front door swung open. Wynn slipped into the shared hallway clutching the spare keys Kim had left with her mother. The old woman's house had been a cinch to break into. The spare keys had been hanging from a hook on the kitchen wall, with a tag labelled 'Kim' helpfully attached. By the time anyone noticed they had been switched with a similar-looking bunch, it would be too late.

Wynn stripped off his jacket, stashed it in his rucksack and pulled on a flimsy coverall, disposable gloves, and overshoes. The lightweight polypropylene fabric made a whiff-whiff sound with every step he took.

There was no burglar alarm to worry about so Wynn's only consideration was the gym freak upstairs. The big Nigerian was a bouncer at a trendy meat market in town and he had fists like wrecking balls. Most days he didn't finish until 3am and frequently slept until midday. So long as nothing stirred him from his slumber Wynn was free to come and go as he pleased.

Another Yale opened the door to Kim's apartment. This was not Wynn's first visit, so he was familiar with the layout. The dreary little flat had been given some much-needed character thanks to a selection of colourful rugs, fairy lights and kooky artwork. Wynn had already carried out a thorough search. Not that there was much to find, other than her diary. It was stashed away in her underwear drawer.

The precious journal was small and pink with a gold clasp. Its pages covered in neat but childlike handwriting. The dots over her i's and j's were tiny circles. Anything of significance was underlined and there was a proliferation of exclamation marks. This was the first time Wynn had enjoyed such unrestricted access to one of his intended victims. There was, after all, only so much to be gleaned from searching through household rubbish and online stalking.

Up until that point, such endeavours had been vital to his success. But in discovering Kim's diary a new dimension had become available. Instead of piecing together scraps of information, he had a spyhole into her most intimate thoughts, feelings, and insecurities.

Kim had good and bad days. Her brightest moments often sprang from the smallest of moments. A smile from one of the old folks. A joke shared with colleagues. Sometimes it could be as simple as buying herself some flowers to freshen up the flat or feeling the sun on her face during a lunch break.

The bad, by comparison, involved sickness, death, or a combination of the two. Ninety per cent of her meanderings were inane bilge but, dotted here and there, were some intriguing nuggets. Kim loved her job, but she was lonely and unfulfilled. She had signed up to various matchmaking sites but had endured a string of disastrous first dates. Having all but given up on finding romance she had taken to masturbating several times a month. She knew it was a perfectly natural thing to do and yet she was plagued with guilt and self-loathing, a by-product of her Catholic upbringing.

Wynn was conflicted by the thought of her pleasuring herself. While he found the act repellent, he enjoyed knowing her secret shame. He flicked through to the more recent entries, keen to stay abreast of her daily musings.

'The strangest thing happened at work today,' she had written. 'Alice's son told me I was "really pretty"!!! I went bright red. I'm so embarrassed!!! His name is Paul. He seems really nice.'

The fact that she was confiding to her diary about him – or rather, his fictitious identity – was encouraging. He closed the book and, taking care not to disturb her neatly arranged bras and panties, returned it to the back of the drawer. He moved to a shelving unit filled with books by celebrity chefs, self-help gurus and writers of the worst kind of trashy fiction.

Along the top shelf was a collection of soft toys. Wynn

plucked an orange-furred monstrosity from the garish menagerie. He opened its mouth to reveal a micro surveillance camera. One of six he had hidden around the flat. Like the others it was motion activated and set to low power to preserve the life of its single lithium battery. It had lasted for almost four weeks but had finally died.

He opened the camera's panel, prised out the power cell and replaced it with another. Then he pushed the camera back into the creature's enormous mouth. Slotting the soft toy into position, between a teddy bear and a tacky unicorn, he adjusted its angle to ensure the fish-eye lens had the best possible view of the room. One down, five to go.

CHAPTER TWENTY

I rritable Bowel Syndrome. That had been Doctor O'Brien's diagnosis. Probably stress related. *Yeah,* thought Ellis Jenrick, *no shit, Sherlock.* Temporary relief came after thirty or forty minutes of straining and groaning. An endeavour that generally left him in a cold sweat and sitting above a nasty mess in the toilet bowl. Not that his GP had the first clue as to why he might be so stressed. Ellis would go to his grave with that knowledge. His conscience had never bothered him before. Now it was devouring his insides like a ravenous tapeworm.

"Come on! Hurry up!"

He was in his bedroom, sat in a gaming chair in front of his top-of-the-range computer. Below the desk his legs jiggled up and down as if they were a pair of hairy pistons. The inside of his mouth was ragged and ulcerated from chewing his cheek. Well-gnawed fingernails drummed the desk as he watched the little blue circle rotate. A tantalising promise of things to come. It was only when his login details were accepted that Ellis felt a familiar blanket of calm envelop him. Finally, he could leave behind the daily grind of his joyless existence and immerse himself in his other life.

Cody spawned in her last-saved location – naked and manacled to a BDSM cross. Her slender limbs were splayed across the wooden X-frame. This one had a range of options available, from hair pulling, and nipple pinching to more extreme forms of sadism and penetration.

Ellis's graphics card was a beast. Its processing power more than capable of handling the movements of his lovingly crafted avatar at the highest resolution. He had spent two years and thousands of pounds in cryptocurrency upgrading Cody's features, skin tone, breasts, and genitalia. She was tall with a well-toned athletic body. Long golden hair, hazel-brown eyes, and a light dusting of freckles across her pretty face. She represented Ellis Jenrick's idea of female perfection – a fifteen-year-old girl.

The avatar had been modelled on his best friend during the early years of secondary school. They had bonded over a shared love of music and their off-beam sense of humour. It had been great. Wonderful in fact. Right up until the moment when everything changed.

As adolescence struck, Cody shed her awkward, beanpole appearance, developed curves and grew in confidence. She was noticed by the older boys. Not only did she relish the attention, she went out of her way to encourage it. Ellis watched from the sidelines as his friend flounced around in a short skirt and tight blouse, smoking, and getting off with lads. She was never so cruel as to blank Ellis, but everything good about their relationship had gone forever.

He slid his cursor over the on-screen Cody, clicked the right mouse button and selected the detach option. One moment the avatar was bound to the cross, the next it was standing. As there was no one else around, he would experiment with a new outfit before teleporting it to a different location. He selected thigh-high latex boots, a tight black corset, and a posture collar.

Ellis winced at an all-too familiar cramp in his guts. It signalled another pilgrimage to the porcelain throne. There was always the option of balancing a laptop on his knees, but a painful defecation was not conducive to arousal. Accepting the inevitable, he grabbed his iPad and trudged into the bathroom. He unbuckled his trousers, pulled down his boxer shorts and settled into position.

While Ellis waited for the cargo bay doors to open, he accessed a Facebook account in the name of Ian Williams. Cody's married name was Hamilton-Brown. Although she had blocked Ellis some time earlier, Ian could still access her timeline. As far as she was aware, Ian was another old friend from her school days. Ian was married to Joanna, and they had two wonderful twin girls, Abby, and Hannah. Cody had no idea that the real Ian Williams did not have a presence on social media, and this was an entirely fictitious account.

Creating and maintaining such a realistic identity took time but was worthwhile. It meant Ellis had a window into Cody's life and could engage in some low-level interaction. Nothing too knowing or familiar. The last thing he needed was her to get suspicious and block this account as well. It was best all around that she believed Ellis Jenrick was no longer stalking her.

The latest batch of photos showed Cody and her square-jawed husband Adam, off on some fancy jaunt to the Maldives. Ellis scrolled through the sun-drenched snaps, dutifully tapping the 'Like' button. God, she looked beautiful in her aquamarine bikini and matching sarong. He saved all but one picture, a solo shot of Adam, to his tablet's memory. Over the years he had spent hours cropping that bellend from his library of images – or more accurately, his shrine.

Look at him, thought Ellis as he vented his bowels, *in his pastel shirt and fucking chinos. What a dickhead!* Ellis began reading the comments section when a notification flashed up at the top of the screen. It was triggered by an app that allowed him to monitor his home security system. The motion-sensitive camera covering the front of his house had been activated. He listened for a moment, waiting for the bell to ring or a knock at the door.

Was someone out there? Creeping around and up to God knows what? The thought of someone attempting to break in or spy on him, triggered an outbreak of goosebumps all over his body. Could it be that nosy old bitch next door? She was always peering at him through her lace curtains, or over the fence.

Thank Christ he had chosen that moment to take a dump, or the intruder might have caught him reaching for the hand lotion. Tapping the icon for his home security app he called up a view of his front garden.

He could barely believe what he saw.

Someone was squatting in the long grass by his living-room window. It looked very much as if they were taking a shit on his property. Ellis coiled out one last stool, wincing from the effort, before wiping his backside. He hoisted up his pants, rinsed his hands then hurried back to the bedroom.

On the monitor, Cody stood by the X-frame, one hand resting on the curve of her hip. In his absence, she was being chatted up by someone whose avatar wore only a wide-brimmed cowboy hat and mirrored sunglasses. Although not exactly subtle, the character's design and body texture was of a suitably high standard. Under normal circumstances Ellis would flirt with the hunky stranger in the hope of being whisked away to some dingy motel or back alley. Alas, such antics would have to wait.

CHAPTER TWENTY-ONE

The ruse had been David's idea. A typically left-field plan from the mind of a writer, but it made sense. Ellis Jenrick would almost certainly recognise David, which meant Frank had to be the decoy. His father-in-law had been less than keen.

"Look," David said, "you're intimidating. There's no getting around it. We can't have him slamming the door in your face or getting spooked and calling the police. That means luring him out by creating a situation that makes him feel territorial. If he sees some random homeless guy squatting on his front lawn, he'll come storming out."

"You hope."

"Yes, I hope, but what would you do?"

"I'd go storming out."

They approached Ellis's house from opposite ends of the road. A few of his neighbours had security cameras but it was easy enough to exploit their blind spots. Frank moved into position but did not have to drop his trousers thanks to the length of his ragged overcoat. He closed his eyes and waited.

Two minutes passed.

Then three.

David watched from a vantage point in the shadows across the road.

As the four-minute mark came and went, Frank felt the muscles in his legs cramp and an uncomfortable twinge flared in his chest. If it had gone on much longer, he would have thrown the towel in, but it was at that moment the front door burst open and he was bathed in light. Ellis stormed out, brandishing a baseball bat.

"You dirty old bastard! Get out of here! Go on! Piss off!"

Frank got to his feet, keeping his eyes fixed on the ground. It was not the first time he had been on the wrong end of a baseball bat.

"Look at me when I'm talking to you!"

After Frank's failed attempt at acquiring a firearm, he had retreated to his workshop. It did not take him long to rustle up the necessary components to build a makeshift stun gun. A battery, a high-voltage generator, an eight-inch length of PVC pipe, some wire, a switch, a couple of bottle caps and the prongs from a two-pin plug.

Frank rammed the business end into the man's neck and jabbed the switch. The sharp crackle lasted a few seconds. Ellis stiffened, as if in the grip of a massive seizure, before dropping the bat and collapsing.

David threw a glance up and down the road to check there was no one around. Satisfied, he pulled a black ski mask over his face. Frank kicked the baseball bat under a hedge, tugged a ski mask over his own face and grabbed Ellis's arms. David took his legs and between them, they bundled their prime suspect inside.

CHAPTER TWENTY-TWO

Ellis was beginning to stir when the last of the zip ties pulled tight around his left wrist. He was in the kitchen, bound to a dining chair.

Frank gave the ridiculous man bun a tug. "Be under no illusion, we're here to cause you pain."

"No..." groaned Ellis. "Please don't—"

"Stop whining. I don't want to hear any begging or pleading. All I want out of you are answers." Frank held up the homemade stun gun and thumbed its switch. Ellis's bloodshot eyes widened as electrical energy crackled between the copper prongs.

"I'll tell you whatever you want to know, just don't hurt me."

"Have you spoken to the police recently?" said David, adjusting his ski mask. It felt uncomfortable. The coarse fabric tight and itchy.

"What?"

"It's a simple enough question. Have you spoken to the police recently? Yes, or no?"

"Yes!"

"Why?"

"A while back I did some work in the village. Something nasty happened there. It was all over the news, but I had nothing to do with it. I'm an engineer. I fit security systems. I was just there to do a job. I don't know anything about the woman who was killed, or that missing kid."

Frank rammed the stun gun into Ellis's shoulder and gave him another zap. Ellis spasmed. His face flushed as his eyes rolled to white. Veins popped in his neck as spittle frothed from his gaping mouth. The man bun slipped free of its knot and whipped the air like a demented rat's tail.

"Just so we're clear," said Frank, his voice an ominous rumble. "I've got all night."

David held out his hand for the stun gun. Frank threw him a quizzical *'Are you sure?'* glance, but his son-in-law nodded, resolute. The device was heavier than the writer had expected but it immediately gave him a sense of power – something he had not felt in a long time. But with it came a trade-off. The mask seemed to grow thicker, tighter, and itchier. Crushing his face and neck like slowly tightening tendrils. Doing his best to ignore the discomfort he pushed the device into Jenrick's groin. "Last chance."

"All right!" his prisoner spluttered. "I'll tell you! I'll tell you everything!"

"Tell me what?"

"I... I sold something."

The dark weave of David's mask curled tighter around his skull. "What did you just say?"

"I sold something. But that's all I did. I swear to God."

"What did you sell?"

"Information. I didn't know anyone would get hurt."

The weight of Ellis Jenrick's sin was etched deep into his face. Snot and spit bubbled from his nose and mouth as he began to sob. David's instinct was to jab the hot switch until the charge ran dry or Ellis lay dead on the floor, whichever came first. The effort to resist that primal instinct was colossal. "What sort of information?" Each word crackled with barely suppressed rage.

"A code to shut down the wi-fi and disable security."

"How does it work?"

"Through an app. You type in the code and the system shuts down. I thought he just wanted to rob the place."

"Who?"

"I don't know."

"I think you do."

"I only know him as Darrian."

"Darrian who?"

"Darrian Hestead. But it's a made-up name. I tried to search for him online but there was nothing."

"How did you meet him?"

"A place I go. It's called Other Life."

Frank balled his hands into fists. "What the fuck are you talking about?"

David gestured for his father-in-law to back down. "Show us."

They dragged Ellis into his bedroom, wooden chair legs scraping parallel trails across the carpet. David settled into the gaming chair and studied an on-screen login prompt.

"What is this? What am I looking at?"

"I must have been kicked out for inactivity. You'll need to log back in."

"How do I do that?"

"Type in the username CodyZero. Capital C. Capital Z. No space. Password candyland99. All lower case."

David tapped in the identifiers and hit Enter. Seconds ticked by which did nothing to ease the tension in the room. Finally, a strange environment appeared. The grim online sex dungeon bustled with a strange cabal. A female avatar sporting a neon pink Mohawk and a huge strap-on dildo was busy pummelling a purple-skinned humanoid from behind. Nearby, a cat-faced dominatrix whipped a bug-eyed gimp. Other denizens amused themselves in similarly depraved ways. Some were naked but most were dressed in bondage gear bedecked with straps, buckles, harnesses, and nipple clamps.

"What is this?" said David, his eyes darting around the screen. "A game?"

"They're avatars controlled by actual people. It's not a game. It's a world."

Frank grabbed Jenrick's rat-tail and yanked his head back. "A world for perverts?"

"No! This is just part of it. You can go to normal places. Museums, zoos, restaurants, the beach. You can visit the Amazon rainforest if that's your thing. Stonehenge. The Pyramids. Easter Island. Wherever you want to go, someone's probably created a version of it. I just enjoy places like... that."

"Because you're a sick bastard?"

"How is it sick? No one gets hurt. It's only pixels."

"Where did you meet Darrian?" David's voice was all business.

"I don't remember."

"I suggest you try."

"There are hundreds of locations like this. Besides, if you want to find him, you'd be better off going to his place. I think he designed it himself. We used to hang out there and chat."

"How do I get there?"

"Click the right mouse button. Under Locations you'll see a list of places I've visited."

"Okay," David said. "What now?"

"There's one called 'The Shades'. See it? Double click and you'll teleport to that location."

David double-tapped the mouse button. The gloomy dungeon dissipated in a kaleidoscopic swirl to be replaced by a new environment. It slowly formed around the Cody avatar. Boxy structures grew in detail. The outline of a road. Streetlights and houses took shape. In the distance was an old-fashioned red telephone box with glass windows. Cody stood naked but for her BDSM gear, on an empty suburban road.

"Can you please put some clothes on her?"

"Her?" Frank's voice was filled with disdain. "It's a cartoon."

"It's not a cartoon! Give her some dignity."

"Dignity! Is he serious?"

"Please!"

David felt as if his head were about to explode through the mask's eye- and mouth-holes. "Fine! What do I do?"

"Right click on her and choose Clothes. There's a whole bunch of options. Just choose something nice."

There were indeed dozens of outfits. From streetwear to formalwear and lingerie to all manner of fetish gear. David selected a sequined cocktail dress and a pair of stilettos.

"Better?"

"Yes. She looks lovely."

"Now what?"

"Use the mouse to control where you look, and the arrow keys to move. Head right, along the road. It's not far."

Controlling the avatar proved to be simple enough, but its coquettish design and sexualised movements were grotesque. David focused on the buildings along either side of the road. They were broadly similar, semi-detached houses. Bleak and featureless. Much like the post-war council houses that could be found up and down the country.

Cody reached a gated play area that was, by comparison to the dreary greys and drab browns of the houses, full of vibrant colour. A red climbing frame shaped like a fire truck. A canary-yellow roundabout. A sky-blue seesaw. On an emerald-green swing sat another avatar. A small boy, aged around eight or nine. It wore brown trousers and a yellow shirt. The only sound that could be heard was the metallic creak of the swing as it arced backwards and forwards.

"This place is for nonces," Frank growled. "Look at it! It's for kiddy-fiddlers!"

"No! That's disgusting. Don't say that."

"So why are you pretending to be a little girl?"

"I'm not!"

"Look at her!" Frank jabbed a finger at the screen. "She's a child."

"I... I..." stammered Ellis. "It's complicated."

"You're a fucking degenerate!"

"Let's take this down a notch." David was equally repulsed but there was nothing to be gained by name-calling.

"How do I talk to him?"

"You can't. He's an NPC."

"A what?"

"A non-player character. He's not controlled by anyone. Just part of the landscape."

"Where do I find this Darrian character?"

"I don't know!"

As well as the slowly constricting mask, David could feel a vein in his temple throb. A sure sign that a blinding headache was not far away. His eyes narrowed as a new rage gripped him. He leapt from his chair and brandished the stun gun an inch from Ellis's face. "How do I find him?"

"I've got no idea. He's not online. Even if he were, I'd only know where he was if he sent me an invite to join him. I can't just track him down. That's not how it works."

David rammed the device into Ellis's cheek. It crackled for

several seconds. Ellis jolted and flushed scarlet. His eyes bulging as if they were about to pop out of his skull.

"This bastard is meticulous," David hissed. "There's no way he would get you to send a security hack through a site like that. It would be logged on a server somewhere. He wouldn't risk it."

Ellis's head lolled sideways, revealing the scorch mark on his face. Drool trickled down his chin as he fixed his aggressors with a glassy-eyed stare.

The pressure around David's head continued to build, as if it were trapped in an iron cage. Screws turning. Bolts tightening. A scold's bridle, he thought, dredging the name from the depths of his memory. An instrument of torture and public humiliation. "Ellis, what is it about this situation you're struggling to understand? Tell us what we want to know, and we'll leave you alone. It's as simple as that."

For the longest moment Ellis said nothing. Then a jagged grin spread across his tear-stained face and he began to laugh.

"What's so funny?"

"I know who you are."

Frank put himself between Ellis and David. "You know nothing."

"I've seen him. I know who he is."

If anything, it was a relief. David seized the opportunity to wrench the ski mask off to reveal his flushed and sweaty face. The stitching had left deep imprints across his skin. "Okay," he said, pausing for a much-needed breath. "Let's start over."

"I'm not telling you anything. Not until I get a guarantee you won't kill me."

Before David could respond, Frank beckoned him into the hallway.

"Open your mouth," David said to Ellis.

"Why?"

"Just do it."

The man in the chair did as he was instructed. David balled up the mask and stuffed it into his captive's mouth, then followed Frank into the hallway.

Frank pulled off his own mask and used it to mop sweat from his forehead.

"What is it?" David's voice was a whisper.

"We can't let him go. Not now."

As his captors spoke in hushed tones, Ellis struggled against his bonds. It was useless. The nylon bindings were too tight. All he had succeeded in doing was to make his wrists bleed. Every nerve ending in his body was still jangling from the shocks to his system. But he had to do something – and fast. With all the strength he could muster, Ellis launched himself backwards.

CHAPTER TWENTY-THREE

David and Frank were back in the bedroom within seconds of hearing the crash. The chair had held firm, despite the impact. Ellis lay on the floor like an upturned turtle. His tears were now more to do with the futility of the situation than any physical pain. David lifted him upright. He removed the gag and stuffed the soggy fabric into his back pocket. "How much?"

Ellis gave him a dumb look, not understanding the question. "What?"

"How much were you paid?"

"Uh... ten thousand."

"Ten thousand what? Pounds? Dollars? Euros?"

"Credits."

"You mean game currency?"

Ellis nodded, averting his eyes.

"What's that in real money?"

The wretched man sobbed as a tsunami of shame crashed over him. He screwed his eyes shut as if he could block out the world.

"I asked you a question."

"About five hundred pounds."

Frank was on him in a second, raining down a volley of crunching blows. Ellis's head whipped from side to side. His cheek split, his bottom lip ripped open, a gash appeared across one eyebrow and the bridge of his nose shattered. Within a minute his face was a glistening scarlet mask.

"That's enough." David spoke quietly but clearly. Frank backed away, his chest heaving from the exertion. "I'll be honest with you, Ellis, there's part of me – a big part – that wants to let him kill you. But more than that, I want my son back. So, if there's anything you can tell us – anything at all – we'll leave you in peace. Yes, you could go to the cops and tell them everything, but I don't think you'll do that. You're a coward. A pathetic nothing of a man. If you talk to the police, then it all comes out. You're an accomplice. An accessory to murder. Everyone will know that you helped Minotaur. Imagine that. How do you think someone like you would get on in prison? Not great I'm guessing."

Ellis's head lolled forward as if he could no longer bear its weight. David grabbed the man's lower jaw and forced it upwards, so they were eye to swollen eye. "Talk to me. Tell me everything."

The words were slurred and distorted by pain. Ellis and the man he knew as Darrian Hestead had met in some anonymous digital sex club. They spent the night chatting and a virtual friendship developed over the subsequent weeks. Talking to this mysterious bull-headed stranger had been easy. Darrian never interrupted, grew bored or judged him. With the benefit of hindsight, Ellis knew it had been a charade. Their friendship, if it could even be called that, had existed only because of where Ellis lived and what he did for a living.

Ellis snorted and coughed up a bloody trail of spittle. "Pen."

David shot a look to Frank who seemed equally confused.

"I need a pen."

David scanned the desk. There was a collection of dust-covered bobble-heads, a pile of magazines and a mug filled with pencils and biros. David plucked one out, pushed it into Ellis's hand then found a scrap of paper. Despite the zip tie, his captive managed to scrawl, *darrianhestead@ol.com*.

"This is how you communicated? By email?"

Ellis managed to nod.

David minimised the screen to reveal an arrangement of typical desktop applications. They were set against a background image of an attractive woman with golden hair and hazel-brown eyes. Scanning the options, David located an email icon. "What's the password?"

Ellis scribbled the word, *labyrinth*.

Heart racing, David typed the word, pressed Enter and that was it, he was in. He had accessed an account created by the killer. But apart from the usual auto-generated messages from the service provider there was nothing in the inbox. David checked the sent mail folder but that too was empty. Nor was there anything in the drafts folder. That was probably how they had communicated.

David knew that when an email is sent it goes down a rabbit hole of servers, routers, and firewalls. It pinballs around the globe leaving a trail of digital breadcrumbs that, with the relevant knowhow, can be traced back to source. That was fine for law-abiding citizens, but a more creative approach was required for anyone looking to maintain a low profile. One such option is to compose an email, save it as a draft and share login details with the person with whom you wish to communicate. They log in, go to the drafts folder and the message will be there, waiting to be read. To reply, the process is repeated. Correspondence can continue back and forth in this way without a single message leaving the account.

But the draft emails were gone.

David checked the deleted items folder but was not surprised to find it had been purged.

Frank's expression was grim. "What now?"

"We cut him loose."

"Are you sure about that?"

David nodded. His head was pounding, and he felt sick. There seemed little point inflicting further pain on this pitiful excuse for a human. They cut their prisoner's bonds and left the house.

CHAPTER TWENTY-FOUR

Frank was already well over the speed limit when he shifted up another gear.

"Frank?" David glanced nervously at his father-in-law. "Slow down."

Seeming not to have heard, Frank slipped into an even higher gear. The truck's engine, thrashed to its limit, screamed as if it were in agony.

There were various reasons why David had not passed his driving test. At the top of that list was confidence. When taking lessons, there had never been a moment when he felt truly safe behind the wheel. He would be on edge the whole time. Expecting a child to run out in front of him or cause a massive pile-up. He had tried various techniques to calm himself, but nothing worked. And so, driving duties fell to Zoe, which was fine. She did not mind, and she was good at it. A careful, considerate, and conscientious road user.

Frank was none of those things.

"Stop the car," David yelled. "Now!"

Frank slammed his foot on the brake. The vehicle screeched

to a halt leaving trails of burnt rubber in its wake. Seatbelts snapped taut as both men jolted forward.

"What the hell's the matter with you?"

As the engine ticked over, Frank stared at a point just beyond the headlight beams. "We should have finished the job. I told you how far we'd have to go. I thought you understood that."

"I'm not a killer."

"What if it had been Minotaur? What then?"

David said nothing. It was a fair question, but he did not have a good answer.

"The little shit's probably talking to the police right now."

"He won't do that."

"How can you be so sure?"

"Like I said... if we go down, so does he."

"I hope you're right because if they come knocking, that's it, we're done. Maybe we should leave it to them after all. We've got nothing."

"I'm not so sure."

Since leaving Ellis Jenrick's house David had been mulling over everything they had discovered. The emails were gone but did that matter? Maybe not.

Frank tossed the ski masks and stun gun onto a bonfire and struck a match. If the police were on their way to arrest them, he was not about to make it easy for them. As the objects crinkled and charred, he strolled back into his house.

David watched the flames grow higher. He had deluded himself into thinking he was ready for such a level of brutality. What they had done was sickening. Some might say evil. Ellis Jenrick was pond life, no one could argue with that, but he deserved a fair trial. To be judged by a jury of his peers and punished appropriately. Most reasonable people would consider that to be a basic human right.

But what about Zoe's rights? She had deserved to live and give birth to their child. Whatever suffering Ellis Jenrick had endured was nothing compared with the atrocities Minotaur inflicted upon his victims.

Frank reappeared holding two mugs. One was chipped. The other was missing its handle. "Get this down you." It was a single malt with a rich and woody fragrance. Frank downed his in one. David sipped his while staring into the crackling fire.

What was it Nietzsche said? 'If you gaze long into an abyss, the abyss will gaze back into you.' As far as David was concerned, the suffering etched upon Ellis Jenrick's face had been that abyss.

CHAPTER TWENTY-FIVE

Only when Ellis was certain his tormentors were gone did he attempt to move. All he could do was slide off the chair, inch by agonising inch. He landed in a heap, staring at the door through eyes that were bloodshot and puffy. It may as well have been a million miles away. And then his bowels opened. There was no warning, flatulence, or the usual ache in his lower intestine. It was just a single expulsion. And no small amount either, judging from the lumpen mass that had settled in his underpants. With the stink of his own faeces invading his nostrils, Ellis Jenrick wept.

The first rays of sunlight were streaming through a gap in the curtains when Ellis woke up – or regained consciousness. He was not sure which. The pain that screamed from every part of his body told him he was still alive – whether he liked it or not. He crawled to the bathroom where, after much fumbling and grunting, he stripped out of his soiled clothes. His vision swam and he lost balance, only just managing to steady himself against the basin. He avoided his reflection. The thought of catching a glimpse of himself was too much to bear. Nor could he bring himself to inspect the areas of frazzled skin where the stun gun had made contact.

He stood under the shower watching his own blood and excrement spiral away down the plughole. When the water became too cold to bear, he twisted the tap into its off position, wrapped himself in towels and limped back to his bedroom.

Calling the police was not an option. His attacker had been right about that. Nor was there any point trying to communicate with the man he knew as Darrian Hestead. When news of Zoe's murder broke, Ellis had tried to make contact, but his messages were ignored. He soon came to view this as a blessing. After all, was it really such a good idea to poke the bear? On balance, probably not. There was only one person he wanted to contact and that was the love of his life.

He logged into Facebook under his pseudonym and called up Cody's home page. It didn't matter how many times he saw her pictures, her face never failed to make him smile, even at the lowest point in his life. Not because she was so pretty, but because of their childhood friendship. He clicked the icon that allowed him to send a direct message. It wasn't something he – or rather Ian Williams – had previously done, so Ellis was presented with a blank canvas. He took a breath and began to type.

Dear Cody,
    I hope you and your family are well. I'm sorry I spoiled everything. You are the nicest person I have ever known, and I wish you all the happiness in the world.
    Your friend,
    Ellis

He read the words through several times. Tweaking here and there until it reflected exactly what he wanted to say and was free of spelling mistakes. Only then did he tap Send.

CHAPTER TWENTY-SIX

Wynn still lived in his childhood home. The aspirations and insecurities of his neighbours had led them to install shiny new composite doors, double glazing, and solar panels. 29 Claremont Road by comparison, had barely changed since it was built in the mid-1950s. An untamed canopy of wisteria fell over the porch and tulip bulbs planted decades earlier bloomed each spring.

He stayed, not out of some misguided sense of loyalty to his mother, or because the property had dropped in value. House prices in that area had rocketed due to their proximity to shops, amenities, and transport links. Wynn had his own reason for staying. It was the same reason no one other than him was allowed to enter the house.

If something broke, he fixed it himself. If it could not be repaired, then it stayed broken. Household chores forever languished at the bottom of his to-do list. He had no reason to decorate, so rooms had barely changed since the previous century. There were the same hideous ornaments everywhere, the same garish wallpaper and gaudy carpets. Elliptical patterns of brown and orange clashing with whorls of yellow and green.

The kitchen walls were decorated in tongued and grooved slats of lacquered pine. They ran vertically, from the skirting to a point twelve inches shy of the textured ceiling. The slats were topped off by a narrow shelf around the room. Occupying every available inch was his mother's egg cup collection. Most were unremarkable, bog-standard designs. Others bore the names of museums, and places of historical interest. One commemorated the late Queen's Silver Jubilee, another celebrated Charles's ill-fated marriage to Lady Diana Spencer. Some were made from cut glass. Others had little legs and comical faces. The only thing they had in common was a thick layer of dust.

One particularly unassuming little egg cup had been hand-painted by the six-year-old Christopher Wynn. A present for his mother's thirtieth birthday. It had been his dad's idea. Father and son had sat together at the dining-room table, cartoons playing on the television in the background. They chatted and giggled as Christopher decorated the cup with blobs of red and yellow paint. It was one of his earliest and fondest memories. A few months later, Dad would be gone. He had kept the affair secret but when his slut fell pregnant, he packed his bags and left. Never to be seen again.

Wynn stood at the Formica worktop chopping a tender cut of meat into equal-sized cubes with a hunting knife. Its four-inch blade was a silvery blur.

His mother had always been prone to mood swings, but the cruelty of abandonment was the final straw. For almost a year, she barely ventured out of the house. Preferring to lay in bed and sob into a pillow. By the age of twelve, Christopher was cleaning the house, doing the shopping, and cooking their meals.

And then Alan had come swaggering into their life.

Wynn glanced down to see the blade resting against the chopping board. On one side of the carbon steel, near the neatly diced meat, lay a thin, almost perfectly circular sliver of flesh.

On the other, a pool of blood formed around the index finger of his left hand. Unbidden thoughts of his stepfather had caused him to lose focus. Without noticing he had sliced the tip of his finger clean off. He placed the knife on the worktop and studied the wound with cold detachment.

Holding his finger over the open jug of a food blender, he watched a crimson droplet lose its fight against gravity. It dripped onto the yolk of a raw egg, one of six already resting on a quart of full-fat milk. The average adult has around ten pints of blood pumping around their body. Wynn knew he could afford to lose around twenty per cent of his quota before experiencing nausea and other mild side effects.

Sure, he thought, squeezing the wound between thumb and forefinger. Why not?

CHAPTER TWENTY-SEVEN

1978

Alan had a gangly frame, horse-like features, and a mop of sandy hair. Young Christopher Wynn's mother used to say it reminded her of the pop singer David Cassidy. While there may have been a grain of truth in her observation, that was where the similarities ended.

As was the style of the day, Alan favoured bell-bottomed jeans, gaudy shirts with wide collars, and a tight-fitting leather jacket. Once he had doused himself with Hai Karate aftershave, Alan believed he was God's gift to women. His charm had certainly worked on Christopher's mum. It was a whirlwind romance, and they were married within a few months. For Christopher, it was a bitter pill to swallow. While he was pleased his mother had a reason to smile again, he was less than happy with her choice of partner. Had it been anyone else, Christopher might have dealt with it better. But there was something about Alan that set wasps buzzing in the boy's stomach.

No one was quite sure how Alan wangled himself a plot on the local allotment. The previous tenant had suffered a massive coronary and died. One minute he had been tending his onion sets, the next he was clutching his chest and convulsing on the floor. When he failed to return home that night his wife of forty years had gone looking for him. She found her beloved spouse lying in a mess of spilt soil and scattered seedlings.

Despite the lengthy waiting list, Alan had wormed his way to the top. When he suggested his stepson might like to help him with the allotment, Christopher's mother was delighted. Finally, the love of her life and her only child would have a chance to bond. And so, one Saturday afternoon, she stood under the wisteria-covered porch and waved them off. A tear in her eye and a warm glow in her heart.

"So, how's school going?" Alan's tone would have curdled milk.

"It's okay."

"Just 'okay'?"

"Yeah."

"Do you like PE?"

"It's all right."

"What about swimming?"

"What about it?"

"Do you like it?"

"Not really."

"Why? I thought all kids like swimming."

"Dunno. I just don't."

"Here, Chrissy..." Alan lowered his tone in a conspiratorial manner. "If you forget your swim trunks, does the teacher make you do it in the nude?"

"No! Why are you asking all these questions?"

"I'm just making conversation. Sorry I asked."

They reached an area where town planners had realised they could not keep building identical semi-detached houses forever. The children's play area consisted of a few swings, a slide, and a climbing frame bolted to the tarmac. The equipment had seen better days. Paint peeled away like scabs to reveal the corroded metal beneath. A skinny boy sat on one of the swings, eyes downcast. His grubby plimsolls scraped across the ground, back and forth. He wore brown corduroy trousers and a mustard-coloured shirt. The clothes were dishevelled, as if he had been rolling around on the floor.

"Hey, I know you," called Alan, "you're Georgie Watt's lad. Robbie, right?"

The boy looked up and nodded. Christopher could tell he had been crying.

"You know my dad?"

"He drinks at The Crown, doesn't he? Me and him are like that." Alan crossed his fingers to indicate what great mates they were. "What happened to you?"

"I was in a fight."

"I hope you gave the other fella what for."

"No." Robbie's voice was forlorn. "He duffed me up."

"Well, you don't want to go home looking like you've been dragged through a hedge backwards. From what I hear, your mum's got a temper on her. Last thing you want is another hiding. Come here. I'll sort you out."

Robbie did as he was told, standing patiently as Alan brushed him down with the palms of his hands. To Christopher it seemed as if his stepfather's fingers had suddenly become abnormally long and splayed out like gnarled twigs. They ran down the boy's arms, chest, stomach and back, repeatedly. When he was finished, Alan produced a steel comb and ran it through Robbie's hair, doing a passable job of flattening it down. "There you go." Alan ran his fingers along the boy's cheek. "Good as new."

Robbie looked up and managed a smile. "Thanks, mister."

"My pleasure. And next time, take my advice – kick him in

the balls and run. He'll think twice about messing with you again."

Alan sent Robbie off with a gentle pat on his backside before returning his attention to Christopher. "See? I'm not that bad, am I?"

They strolled along a litter-strewn alleyway. The cloying stink of urine hung heavy in the air. The stench was so bad that Christopher had to pinch his nose between thumb and forefinger to block it out. Alan seemed not to notice. In fact, he had developed a spring in his step since encountering young Robbie. He whistled some jaunty pop tune, although it was not one Christopher recognised.

The alleyway opened onto a busy road leading to a parade of shops. A racist slogan was daubed in red paint across the newsagent's window. Someone had tried scrubbing it off but succeeded only in smearing it around, making it ten times worse. To the left was the petrol station where Christopher's mother took her Mini when it needed filling up with two-star, or to get it repaired. Directly across the road, beyond a row of beech trees, were the allotments. An oasis of green amongst the drab suburban sprawl.

Alan and Christopher waited for a break in the traffic before crossing the road. Foregoing the actual entrance, they skipped over a shallow ditch, ducked through an opening in the chain-link fence, onto a well-trodden dirt path. It ran around the allotment's perimeter, occasionally branching off at right angles to provide a route through the plots. A birds-eye view would have shown the area to be divided into equal parcels of land. Each measured about the size of a tennis court and no two looked the same. Many were ablaze with colour from a dazzling array of lovingly tended flowers.

Christopher knew a rose when he saw one but other than that he could not tell a peony from a petunia. He could however appreciate their beauty. They passed a wiry octogenarian who was digging over a vegetable patch, hardly breaking a sweat. He wore a moth-eaten cardigan over a shirt and tie. The old man spotted Christopher and gave him a gummy smile. Elsewhere, another elderly gent puffed on a briar pipe while enjoying the sun's warmth on his wrinkled face.

Christopher had not known what to expect from this Saturday afternoon sojourn. But looking around at this strange new wonderland, with its prize-winning marrows and towering sunflowers, a feeling of tranquillity descended upon him. Could the journey have been worth it after all?

Alan glanced back and spotted the awe on Christopher's face. "It's quite something isn't it?"

Christopher nodded. "It's really nice."

"My plot's just up there. Come on, chop-chop!"

They followed the pathway until it took a sharp left turn. With a theatrical sweep of his hand Alan indicated they had arrived. "Ta-da!"

He maintained his poise, as if he were a snake-oil salesman in the Old West presenting some new remedy for all known maladies. "What do you think?"

Christopher's brow crinkled, unsure how to respond. What had once been a vegetable patch was overrun with thorny brambles and a jungle of waist-high nettles. Three bamboo wigwams were cocooned in a tangle of long-dead runner beans, bone white in the afternoon sun. Christopher looked from his stepfather's plot to those on either side. Although far from being among the best-tended they at least showed signs that effort had been made.

"Come and have a look inside the shed."

The structure was so dilapidated a light breeze might have brought the whole thing crashing down. Its roof was a sheet of corrugated iron, patched up with tarpaulin and chicken wire. A single pane of glass occupied the brittle window frame. The view inside obscured by newspaper. Clouds of mosquitos drifted lazily in the air above a barrel of stagnant rainwater. Nearby was a rusty wheelbarrow, a watering can, and the blackened remains of a bonfire. As if by contrast, the rickety door was held in place by a shiny brass padlock hanging from a sturdy hasp. Even to Christopher's young eyes this attempt at securing the rickety shed seemed over the top.

Alan flashed an ingratiating smile as his big thumbs worked the padlock. It had a combination consisting of four numbers. He rolled the tumblers into their correct sequence and the shackle sprung free. "Open sesame!"

He pocketed the padlock, opened the door, and entered the shed.

The brief spell of calm Christopher had felt upon reaching the allotment was gone and the wasps had come swarming back. They were buzzing even louder than ever.

Wynn allowed a final crimson bead to join the other red-spotted ingredients before patching himself up. He used half a cotton-wool ball and a strip of fabric plaster from the first aid kit. It was from the same tin his mother had always gone to whenever he, as a child, had grazed a knee or scraped an elbow.

Wynn tipped the glistening cubes of meat, and the sliver of his own fingertip into the jug. Twisting the cap into position he set the gloopy mix roaring into life. The contents were quickly whipped into a pink mush. Wynn watched the protein tornado for a full sixty seconds before shutting off the power. He detached the jug and poured the frothy mix into a sippy cup.

His guest's supper was ready.

CHAPTER TWENTY-EIGHT

Frank gave David a lift into Carlton Bridge and dropped him off along the bustling high street. It had a reasonable selection of shops, and within an hour David had purchased a new set of clothes and a swanky laptop. He checked into The Ambassador, a shining beacon of above-average hospitality.

The receptionist greeted David with a dazzling smile and a genial welcome. How much time had he spent in near-identical accommodation over the years? Or more to the point, how had he allowed book tours to consume such a large chunk of his life? So many wasted days that could have been spent with Zoe and Charlie. Having fun, making memories and above all, keeping them safe. The part of his brain which handled guilt was on overdrive as he entered the lift. If he had any hope of figuring out his next move, he would need to remain objective. He could not afford to let his already tenuous grip on things slip.

His room was clean and comfortable. Not that he required luxury, he just needed somewhere quiet, with wi-fi and coffee. He showered and changed into his newly purchased clothes. Jeans, T-shirt, hoodie, and a pair of high-top trainers. It was the sort of combination Zoe would choose for him in an attempt at shedding his 'Harvard College Professor' appearance. 'A bookish Clive Owen.' That's what she used to call him. When dining with friends, she would often tease her husband, saying that until the actual Clive Owen became available, David would just have to do.

He rang through to reception and ordered room service. His food arrived forty minutes later but he barely tasted the burger and chips. It was fuel for the engine, no more than that. He gnawed his fingernails as the laptop ran through its installation process. When it was connected to the hotel's wi-fi, he unfolded the sketch he had made of Minotaur's labyrinth.

Using a complimentary pen, David drew a line representing the only route through the maze. It stretched upwards, turned left, went upwards again before turning right, then down, then left again into the central chamber. It resembled a hook, or perhaps an inverted question mark. Was that significant? Did the labyrinth's internal geography carry some hidden cipher? In its walls perhaps, or the negative space between them? Or was the true meaning so warped it could only be interpreted by its architect?

And what of Other Life, the virtual world in which Ellis Jenrick and Darrian Hestead had first crossed paths? Something had been bugging David since teleporting the hyper-sexualised avatar to the location known as 'The Shades'. Ellis said it had been created by Hestead, in which case it had to be important. But in what way?

David googled Other Life and followed a link to the website. The home page had a sleek design. *Meet amazing new people and explore a world beyond your imagination* proclaimed the blurb. An animated showreel presented enticing images of beautifully designed avatars exploring exotic locations.

A pair of lovers strolled hand in hand along a tropical beach. A group of friends socialised on the moonlit veranda of a clifftop nightclub. There were many others, although none depicting an underage girl chained to a bondage cross. Before he could log on it was necessary to install the software. David set the download going and watched the percentage bar creep towards its end point.

Jenrick's username was CodyZero. Capital C. Capital Z. No space. But what about the password? David trawled his memory but came up short. It had ended with a double nine, he was sure of that much. Was it Cody99?

No, not Cody.

Candy.

Yes. The password was Candy something or other. But what?

Candycrush?

That was close but not quite right.

Candybar? Candystripe? Candyland?

Yes. That was it. The password was candyland99. All lower case.

CHAPTER TWENTY-NINE

There was a steely determination in Rybak's expression as she approached her old office. Loveday was on the phone, giving some poor sod a bollocking. She waited for him to slam down the handset before knocking. The burly investigator beckoned her in, still fuming from the call.

"If it's not convenient, Guv–"

"What do you want?"

She was irritated to see her notoriously cluttered desk had been tidied. Even the bedraggled spider plant on the windowsill looked healthier than usual. Almost as if someone had bothered to water it. "Guv, I think we should go back to basics."

"You're not happy about the way I'm running things?"

"I didn't say that."

"Nevertheless, the subtext is there, and received loud and clear. Look, whatever you may think of me, I've been living and breathing this case for almost a year. As much as it sticks in my throat to say, we're dealing with one clever bastard." His nostrils flared. A micro gesture that told Rybak her gut instinct was right. Loveday was a spent force.

"With all due respect–"

The senior detective stifled a laugh.

"Did I say something amusing?"

"Just get to the point."

"The way he's been second-guessing us... is it possible he's ex-job?"

"It's possible, yes. And you're not the first to suggest that. We've even carried out some data modelling on that very scenario. It's worrying to see how so many of our people have ended up. Burnouts. Shut-ins. Alcoholics. Wife-beaters. Rapists. There was one guy, a forty-seven-year-old duty sergeant down in Worthing. He sliced his wife's throat, put a pillow over his daughter's face, snapped the dog's neck and then went for a pint at his local. Can you imagine that? So many names. So many depressed, desperate souls but not one damn thing connecting any of them to the Minotaur case."

"So, we just keep grinding the same old gears, do we?"

"Unless you have any genius ideas you'd like to share."

"I think we should take another look at how the killer gained access to the Knights' cottage."

"I'm listening."

"He knew the husband would be away and that bad weather would disrupt the search. He also knew about the security system."

"Yes. And...?"

"It's not his usual MO. Three other victims had cameras and alarms installed, but nothing as sophisticated as the Knights' system. They were all killed away from their homes. Remotely deactivating the Emperor 5 isn't standard knowledge. You can't just watch a YouTube video. Which makes me think it's not the killer's field of expertise."

"Are you suggesting he had an accomplice?"

"I don't think we can rule it out."

"But he would still have needed Zoe Knight to open the

front door. Surely that would have been less likely if there were two people, potentially both male, standing on her doorstep."

"Maybe the second person was hidden from view. Or maybe the information was passed along beforehand. Whichever way it played out we know Zoe put the chain on the front door. She did everything right. She just didn't expect her attacker to come with bolt cutters."

Loveday leant back, mulling this over. He locked hands behind his head revealing damp circles in the armpits of his lime-green shirt. "Okay. Have another little chat with Mr Jenrick. Just don't push him too hard. At least, not yet."

CHAPTER THIRTY

S pending several hours on what was essentially a computer game felt wrong when the stakes were so high. It was a leap of faith, and David knew it, but he could not shake the feeling that somewhere in the online world was a clue to Minotaur's identity or whereabouts.

Guiding the Cody avatar from place to place made him feel queasy. The character's underage design, body shape, even the way she walked felt wrong on so many levels. In his books, David had written about all manner of steamy encounters. Passionate love affairs, infidelity, incest and even an orgy or two, but nothing that came close to Ellis Jenrick's sick fantasy. But whether David liked it or not, Cody was his pathfinder through this strange place.

His theory had been that The Shades replicated Minotaur's labyrinth. Roads were pathways and the semi-detached houses were its walls. He dropped that idea when it became obvious the area was nowhere near as large as it seemed. The on-screen horizon turned out to be a collision mesh that prevented exploration beyond a certain point. Upon reaching this invisible barrier, the avatar's feet glided in place, as if on a treadmill. The houses were similarly devoid of options. Despite their exterior detail it was impossible to venture past the front gates or interact with anything of interest within their boundaries.

David studied a map he had sketched on hotel stationery. It showed the streets, houses, a children's play area, a narrow alleyway, a parade of shops and the one section he had yet to explore – an expanse of land filled with greenhouses, sheds, and runner-bean frames. If there were secrets to be found, it had to be in there. First though, he needed another caffeine hit.

David tore open the last sachet of instant coffee and poured freeze-dried granules into a mug bearing the hotel logo – the letter 'A' in a fancy gold font. As the kettle gurgled into life, he crossed to the window to look outside. It was 1am. The Irish pub across the road had long since called last orders. Nor were there any lights on at the Jewel of India restaurant. Apart from a flicker of neon from The Green Baize Snooker Club and a twinkle of headlights on the outskirts of town, Carlton Bridge had an eerie stillness. It was not a million miles away from the virtual domain David had been exploring. Was it possible The Shades was based on a view familiar to Minotaur? If so, why would he go to all the effort of replicating it in a digital format?

Unless...

The word loomed large in David's mind. Two syllables that can turn the world on its axis. Unless...

The kettle reached boiling point. It clicked off, steam drifting lazily from its spout. David's eyes remained fixed on the view outside. Minotaur was not prone to slip-ups. If some real-world version of The Shades existed, then surely there was only one explanation. Minotaur *wanted* someone to make the connection. The small hairs on the back of David's neck went rigid.

The maze was a challenge. Minotaur's way of throwing down the gauntlet, seeking a worthy opponent. No wonder the police looked so incompetent. All they had to go on was the evidence, due process, and a need to establish a burden of proof. Unless they understood the killer's online presence, what chance did they have?

Other Life had hundreds of thousands of members, with new people joining the community every day. The Shades was just one of many locations – a virtual needle hiding in a digital haystack. A maze within a maze.

Leaving the kettle untouched, David hurried back to the computer and googled 'The Shades, United Kingdom'. It was a long shot, and he was not surprised to see a list of companies – most of which were pubs, clubs, bars, and restaurants – whose trading name contained the word 'Shade' or 'Shades'. Could 'The Shades' be an abbreviation, a nickname used by residents or was it the product of a madman's crazed imagination?

David switched back to Other Life. He guided Cody along a narrow alleyway, across a road lined with beech trees, to an iron gate through which the allotment could be glimpsed. David clicked on the entrance and chose the only available option – Open. The gate swung aside, and the avatar sashayed through.

The change was immediate.

Cody was no longer walking but falling. Her arms pinwheeling as she plummeted through a blank sky. Her previous environment had blinked out of existence, and she was heading towards some unseen landing point far below. David tapped keys randomly, desperately trying to reverse what was happening. "Shit! Shit! Shit!"

He had little choice but to sit back and watch as Cody fell. There was no dying in Other Life so when she eventually landed, she simply stood up and dusted herself off. Her new environment was an empty lot. Pale terrain unencumbered by texture and detail. David called up the list of saved locations and clicked The Shades. It prompted a message in a crisp white font to appear on-screen.

The site owner has blocked you from this location.

CHAPTER THIRTY-ONE

Wynn stared at his monitor. The index finger of his right hand still rested on the mouse button he had just clicked to expel the intruder. Why had Ellis Jenrick's sickeningly childlike avatar returned to The Shades? It made no sense. Their association was over and had been for some time. Was he so infatuated that, after everything, he harboured thoughts of a reconciliation?

Opening the site maintenance screen, Wynn changed the permissions to invitation only. If Jenrick tried to sneak back using an alternate identity, he would hit an invisible wall and bounce off into the nearest sandbox.

Wynn's train of thought was derailed by an insistent noise from the next room. Despite lagging the walls with foam rubber tiles his guest still managed to create a low-level racket from time to time. Not that Wynn was concerned. The noise was not enough to attract the attention of an inquisitive neighbour or passers-by. Besides, at such a late hour, the only living things not tucked up in bed were the urban foxes. Wynn often watched them from his bedroom window as they skulked around in the dead of night. Bony creatures with vicious grins and eyes that flashed silver in the darkness. There was a fascinating duality about them. Cautious but graceful. Feral but majestic. Intriguing but dangerous. Wynn could not help but feel a connection.

The dull sound from the room next door continued. Usually, he would have taken steps to silence his guest. There were a range of options at his disposal. From drugs and ball gags to blunt instruments and bladed weapons. But he was anxious to re-enter the labyrinth so thoughts of a suitable punishment would have to wait.

Wynn's Other Life avatar had the cobblestone physique of a steroid-ingesting muscleman. It wore skin-tight leather trousers and heavy boots crested with death-head skulls. The creature was bare-chested. Bulging pecs glistened as if smeared with baby oil. Completing his digital persona – the pièce de résistance – was the head of a bull. There were many bull-headed men to be found prowling the virtual bars and clubs but none quite like this.

It was a unique creation. The best that credits could buy. It had a pair of huge curling horns, and a narrow snout with nostrils that flared from time to time. The work of an anonymous coder. One of many to ply their skills through Other Life.

There was money to be made in creating bespoke items for those wanting to stand out from the crowd. Trinkets and emblems celebrating online love affairs. Whole body tattoos for the Yakuza gangs of downtown New Tokyo. From clothing to genitalia, for the right price anything and everything could be coded into existence.

Calling this godlike creation 'Minotaur' had seemed too obvious. Instead, Wynn had opted for something incongruous that bore a hidden meaning that only he could enjoy. The creature he had named 'Darrian Hestead' stalked through the digital allotment. Its on-screen depiction was as ugly and weed infested as it had been all those years ago. When he reached the shed, he typed in a four-digit password and stepped inside.

Wynn's avatar stood in a high-ceilinged corridor. It was designed to look as if it were constructed from sandstone blocks. Wall-mounted brackets held flickering torches. Their flames washed the route ahead in an eerie tangerine glow.

In Greek mythology, the architect and craftsman Daedalus designed a maze to imprison the Minotaur. Wynn had created his own version using Other Life's proprietary developer tools. Its layout mirrored his own design. Textures were based on images he had found while trawling the internet. Mazes and mausoleums from the ancient world to make it appear as if it were hand built by a thousand slaves. As he created this realm of grids and vectors, Wynn imagined himself cracking a whip across the withered backs of his half-starved minions.

The Shades had taken him the best part of a year to complete. It had been his sandpit. A space in which to learn and practise new coding skills. Only when it was finished to the highest standard had he begun working on the labyrinth. It became his obsession. Sometimes labouring day and night. Often neglecting to wash or feed himself. Always striving for perfection. Studying every pixel, and every frame from every angle.

There could be no short cuts with this endeavour. No concessions. No compromise. It had to be right. He owed that much to his twelve-year-old self. That was when he had drawn his first tentative sketch of the maze. There had been many aborted attempts in those early days. The waste bin in the corner of his bedroom was often crowned with balled-up sheets of A4.

Wynn had replaced his desk and chair since then and stashed his toys in the loft. He still had the same rust-brown carpet and musty curtains, but the hideous, bottle-green wallpaper had been stripped away to reveal the plaster beneath. Much of it was covered in pencil sketches and paintings of the maze. The largest was huge, messy, and covered an entire wall.

Wynn had used his hands rather than brushes to render the design. Angry strokes in dark hues of purple and red were clearly the product of a disturbed mind. In pride of place above the bed was his original drawing. A maze he had sketched in pencil more than forty years previously. The paper had, at one stage, been folded into eighths, and although discoloured, its lines remained clear.

During its creation, young Christopher came to understand that a maze can fail for many reasons. If a pathway is too narrow or there is one blind alley too many, the design becomes skewed and ugly. Space, balance, and symmetry must be judged to perfection. The challenge, as with so many things in life, was to create a route to the centre that was hidden in plain sight.

Wynn guided his avatar along the branching corridors, making slow but steady progress towards the central chamber. There were no more tweaks to be made. He was content with the textures, the geometry, and the lighting. His avatar's footsteps even had a pleasing echo as the bull-headed creature stalked along the corridors.

His twelve-year-old self could not have imagined that one day, the place to which he had retreated in his darkest moments, would be brought to life in such glorious detail.

CHAPTER THIRTY-TWO

1**978**
Christopher and Alan sat on a pair of rusty fold-out picnic chairs. A transistor radio on the workbench played a succession of crackly disco tunes on its AM frequency. Alan was talking about his favourite bands. Jethro Tull. Fleetwood Mac. Pink Floyd. Their strange names meant nothing to Christopher. He had no interest in what pioneering technology, experimental instruments, or mind-altering substances had been involved in their recording process. Unaware of his stepson's indifference, Alan continued, as if the boy were hanging on his every word.

"Right," he said eventually, "I'm off to the Paki shop for some ciggies. You'll be all right here for ten minutes, won't you?"

Christopher nodded. He would rather be alone with no one to talk to and nothing to do than listen to Alan for another second.

"Good boy. Tell you what, I'll get you a comic and some sweeties. How does that sound, eh?" Without waiting for an answer, he hoisted himself out of the chair and left the shed.

Christopher looked around the dingy interior, checking out

the cobwebby nooks and crannies. The only residual sign of a previous occupant was the faint silhouette of tools on the far wall. An impressive selection of hammers, screwdrivers, pliers, and spanners. His eyes shifted to the window. The glass was covered by sheets of newspaper.

From the outside, an article about the world's first test-tube baby could be seen. On the inside, however, was a black-and-white photograph of a bare-chested lady with long curly brown hair. He had never seen a naked woman before. Not even an accidental glimpse of his mother getting dressed in the morning, or ready for bed at night. The sight of the woman's huge breasts made him feel uncomfortable and yet he could not look away. Why wasn't she wearing any clothes? Why had she allowed herself to be photographed like that? And what did she have to be smiling about? None of it made any sense.

He was still staring at the picture when Alan returned. "Do you like girls, Chrissy?"

Christopher looked around, startled. His stepfather stood in the doorway, casually smoking a cone-shaped cigarette. There was something different about him. His eyes were glassy and heavy-lidded. His pupils much wider than usual. The look on his face set the wasps buzzing again. "I asked you a question, Chrissy. Do you like girls?"

Christopher shook his head, no.

"Very wise," said Alan, taking a long drag on the spliff. "They're all sluts."

The boy didn't know what that word meant, but it didn't sound very nice.

Alan stepped into the shed, pulling the door closed behind him. Rather than sit down or lean against the workbench he made a point of blocking the only way out.

"What about me, Chrissy? Do you like me?"

Christopher shrugged.

"Come on, be honest. You don't like me, do you? That's fine, I get it. You want your real dad back but I'm afraid that's not going to happen. He's gone for good. Why? Because of a slut."

With the door closed the cannabis smoke lingered in the enclosed space. Christopher could not help but breathe it in.

"Unlike your old man, I'm going nowhere. You won't catch me messing about with some little whore. It's just me and your mum. Oh, and you, of course. She's a good woman, your mum. I mean, she's got her problems..." he paused to tap the side of his head, "but she's not like the others." Smoke curled from his mouth as he spoke. Christopher felt woozy and wanted to go home.

"The thing is, Chrissy, as you get older, you'll come to realise there are certain things that a woman is supposed to do for her man. It's their duty. Your mum does some of those things, but not others." He slid one hand into his trouser pocket. Christopher could see it, shifting around, under the fabric, moving from side to side.

"The way I see it, if she's not prepared to put herself out, you'll have to do it instead. I've got to clean out the dirty water somehow, haven't I?"

Christopher did not know what his stepfather meant, but the funny smell was making him feel sleepy. Alan took a final drag before crushing the discoloured roach underfoot. "Get on your knees."

He dragged the boy off the chair and manhandled him into a kneeling position. His hands moved to his belt to unclasp the ornamental buckle. It was a bull. Made from bronze and tarnished with age. Curling horns, narrow eyes and a broad snout set in a vicious snarl.

The relentless beat of a Moog synth pulsed from the radio as Alan forced his stubby cock into the boy's mouth. It tasted bad. Oily secretions from an unwashed foreskin. Alan moaned as something hot and salty filled Christopher's mouth. The pervert shuddered and moaned as his long fingers clawed the child's hair.

"Hmmm," he murmured, withdrawing his wilting member. "Good boy."

Only when he had zipped himself up did he cast a look at the desperate wretch at his feet. Tears welled in Christopher's eyes as pearly white fluid oozed down his chin.

"This will be our little secret," said Alan. "You can keep a secret, can't you?"

CHAPTER THIRTY-THREE

It was over. Time for David to go back to Oldcroft Lane and put aside all thoughts of finding Charlie himself. What had he been thinking? He was no gun-toting heavy. He was an author and history geek. More at home in a library than out in the big bad world.

Leave it to the police.

The words clanged in his mind. Despite his misgivings, realistically it was the only sensible course of action. Maybe they would finally get their act together and uncover some vital clue that unlocked the case.

David knocked back the last of the miniature whisky bottles. The minibar had been raided soon after he was kicked out of The Shades. It had not taken him long to consume the tins of lager and work his way through the little bottles of red and white wine. Then he had turned his attention to the spirits.

The room was spinning and there was a good chance he would throw up but fuck it. He had mixed his drinks which meant he could expect a thumping headache the next day but fuck it. In fact, he thought, fuck it all to Hell. He hurled the empty miniature across the room.

The bottle smashed against the wall in a starburst of glittering fragments. Shards covered a faux suede club chair and peppered the carpet nearby. But it was not enough – the rage was still there. Rattling the bars of its cage and screaming for release. David staggered to the desk, picked up the laptop in a two-handed grip, raised it above his head and brought it down hard against the desktop.

Thwack!

Someone in the next room thumped on the wall but fuck it.

David tossed the computer aside. As it hit the floor the keyboard fell away to reveal a spider's web of fractures across the screen. He swept his arm across the desk in a wide arc. Stationery, a mug, a menu, a Do Not Disturb sign, a pen, laminated fire drill instructions and an advertising pamphlet fell to the carpet. A load of crap bearing the hotel's logo – a golden 'A' in a fancy font.

Now that he looked, he could see it everywhere. Stitched into the carpet. Embroidered into the curtains. Emblazoned on the breast pocket of a fluffy dressing gown. He had never hated a single letter so much in his life.

The rumpus triggered another barrage of angry thumps from the next room. David responded by smashing the wall with the palm of his hand. The effort triggered a wave of nausea that sent him dashing to the toilet. Within seconds a spray of foul brown fluid exploded from his mouth and hit the water.

When there was nothing left, his fingers patted the cistern until they found the push-button flush. Giving it a jab, he watched the vomit spiral away. He tore off a few sheets of toilet paper – also covered in little golden A's – to blow his nose.

Was this how the rest of his life would play out? Pity drinking to the point of sickness. It seemed that way but fuck it.

David returned to the bedroom and surveyed the mess. There was a jagged stain on the wall, broken glass on the furniture and a load of hotel crap on the floor. Retrieving a dustpan and brush from the cupboard he set about sweeping up the glass. The rage had been replaced by its equally unpleasant sibling, shame. He emptied tiny shards into the bin then turned his attention to the fallen items.

David gathered them up and arranged the items back on the desk, in a crude approximation of their original positions. He slotted the advertising pamphlet between the back of the phone and the wall, but it did not stay there for long. Instead, it slid sideways and slipped behind the desk to land by the skirting. David knelt to retrieve the pamphlet. Still groggy from the booze he opened the glossy trifold and attempted to focus.

He caught a few words here and there. Something about high-quality amenities and commitment to customer service. It was the usual marketing bumph that described most halfway-decent hotels. There were pictures of a restaurant, a gym, and a sauna. Minimum requirements for most of their customers. The pamphlet wasn't telling him anything he needed to know so why was he still staring at it, as if the text contained hidden secrets?

Then it hit him. Like Saul on the road to Damascus, scales fell from his eyes, and he could finally see. On the back page was a detail-free outline of the British Isles. What distinguished this map were the little golden A's that were dotted up and down the country. Each one denoted the location of an Ambassador Hotel. There were clusters in London and the north-east, while elsewhere was more sporadic.

David had seen a similar map only recently. It wasn't glossy like this one, and instead of little golden A's it was covered in black dots. It formed part of his father-in-law's sprawling wall collage and pinpointed the location of twelve murders attributed to Minotaur.

CHAPTER THIRTY-FOUR

I t was the dawn chorus that usually woke Bibi Whistler. She
didn't mind the melodic tweets and chirrups of the starlings
outside. It was a pleasant enough way to ease herself into
another day of rose tea, crossword puzzles, and keeping a
watchful eye on her neighbours. The thrum of an idling car
engine came as an unwelcome shock to her well-attuned system.
She fumbled around on the bedside cabinet for her thick-
rimmed glasses and squinted at the alarm clock. According to
the big red numbers it was 4.34am.

Bibi pushed aside her floral duvet and threw back the
curtains. Misty sunlight gave the view from her bedroom
window a hazy filter. As if the world outside had yet to slip into
focus. There was no one around but that was to be expected. It
was too early for the milkman or the first of the dog walkers. She
peered left and right, craning her head for the best angle up and
down the street. There was the usual selection of cars parked in
driveways, but they were all dormant.

Very odd, she mused. Very odd indeed.

The man next door kept his van locked away in the garage at
night. He had even installed a heavy duty security bar to

prevent tampering. Bibi had always thought there was something odd about him. He often kept his blinds shut during the day, and the pathetic little rat-tail perched on top of his head was simply ludicrous. If the noise continued, she would have no choice but to call the police.

CHAPTER THIRTY-FIVE

Frank sped back to Ellis Jenrick's house. As far as he was concerned, the snivelling little toerag had signed his own execution order. There could be no forgiveness and no mercy. Frank would however ensure it was quick and painless.

David had shown himself to be more capable than Frank could have imagined. But torturing Ellis was one thing. Killing him was another matter entirely. It represented a moral line David would not cross. If anything, it made him normal. Unlike Frank, he was a good man at heart.

During his time working for Eddie Grand, Frank had proven himself to be a loyal foot soldier. He carried out instructions without question and built a reputation as someone who got the job done, whatever it took. He had been a force of nature. A human battering ram. The people he beat up and tortured had all deserved it, with one exception – a man named Gary Starr. How could that be the name of a security guard? It seemed more appropriate for the lead singer in a glam rock band. Yet there it was, printed on an ID badge pinned to his breast pocket.

Frank had used a crowbar to smash the man's hand. The

sound of its impact still haunted him. Grisly high-pitched crunches playing on an endless loop. Frank often reflected on how much further he would have gone that day. For instance, making good on his threat of setting the man alight. Thankfully, Gary Starr had seen sense, telling the gang where to find the key they needed. In the darkest pit of his soul, Frank knew that had it been necessary, he would not have thought twice about dousing Gary in petrol and striking a match.

Parking a few streets away Frank returned to Jenrick's house. The last thing he expected was to find the road cordoned off and a crowd of neighbours milling around. David had been wrong. The cops must have been called after they left. Frank cursed himself. He should have gone with his instinct and killed the bastard there and then.

"What's going on?" he asked one of his fellow gawkers, a sporty woman in her late thirties. She wore baby pink jogging gear and trainers. Her chestnut hair tied back in a ponytail. "I don't know," she said between swigs from a water bottle. "But it doesn't look good."

CHAPTER THIRTY-SIX

In his relatively short time as a police officer, Detective Sergeant Vikram Prakesh had seen his share of corpses. This, however, was a first for him. Ellis Jenrick had been dead for five hours by the time the Senior Fire Officer deemed it safe for the police and paramedics to enter the garage. Prakesh remained outside as a stretcher team removed the body.

Jenrick had been sitting in the driver's seat of his Vauxhall combo van. The security engineer had turned the vehicle into a gas chamber. A length of hosepipe inserted into the exhaust pipe, secured with duct tape, and fed through the top of the driver's side window. The narrow gap had been sealed with more tape. Jenrick had started the engine and left the motor running until he was overcome by carbon monoxide fumes.

The crime-scene photographer fired off multiple shots from various angles. When he was finished the paramedics lifted the body onto a gurney. Jenrick's face was the colour of minced beef and speckled with dark lesions.

"Does that look normal to you?" asked Prakesh.

The paramedics exchanged an eye-rolling glance. The young detective knew from bitter experience it meant Dumb

Cop alert. "What I mean is, look at his face. There seems to be some bruising. Is that usual for CO_2 poisoning? And there..." He indicated the welt on Jenrick's cheek. "Could that be a burn mark?"

"Possibly," said the first paramedic. "But it's best not to jump to conclusions."

A blanket was pulled over Jenrick's cherry-red face before they loaded him into the ambulance. Prakesh joined the crime-scene photographer who was taking pictures of the vehicle. Along its side was a neat vinyl decal of the company's name – Trinity Home Security Services – along with its logo, website, social media, and telephone number.

"When they're ready," said Prakesh, "do me a favour and send the jpegs over."

"Will do."

Prakesh emerged from the garage, mulling over the circumstances of Jenrick's sudden passing. The plan had been to bring him back in for questioning but now he was dead. Coincidence? It seemed unlikely. Prakesh was poised to call Rybak when he spotted a familiar face amongst the assembled rubberneckers – Frank Crocker. Their eyes met, and Prakesh was certain he saw a flash of guilt.

Frank hurried across the road into Morton Lane. He walked faster than usual, anxious to put as much distance as possible between himself and Prakesh. Glancing over his shoulder he saw the young detective was following him. A police radio held to his mouth as if he were calling for backup.

The truck was parked halfway along the road, under the shadow of a silver birch. If Frank were to continue at his current pace he would be detained before he reached the vehicle. His only option was to run. Arms and legs pumping, he dashed past a shaggy Leylandii. Overhanging ferns whipped his face as he risked another look back. Prakesh had broken into a sprint and was gaining ground, fast.

Frank soon realised he had overestimated his own stamina. His joints stiffened and his attempt at running became an awkward, lolloping gait. More worrying was the growing pain in his chest. He gasped for breath and slowed to a walking pace. With every step the truck seemed to recede further into the distance. As if on autopilot he reached for his keys but was all fingers and thumbs.

"Mr Crocker? Are you all right?"

Frank went limp and fell sideways. He hit the pavement, his forehead taking the brunt of the impact. Prakesh rolled him over onto his back and moments later began chest compressions. "Stay with me, Frank!"

But Frank's thoughts were elsewhere. It was Zoe's third birthday. He and Lucy, along with family and friends, were crowded around to watch the little girl blow out the candles on her cake.

Zoe looked adorable in her pink party dress and hair tied in bunches. She took a deep breath and blew as hard as she could. But it wasn't just the three dainty flames that were snuffed out. The whole world went black.

CHAPTER THIRTY-SEVEN

David checked out of the Ambassador and settled the bill for his ill-advised raid on the minibar. He had a thumping headache and a sour taste that minty fresh toothpaste could do nothing to shift. After grabbing an Americano from an overpriced coffee shop, he spotted a community hub across the road. Posters taped to its windows advertised support groups, adult education, and free internet.

David found an available workstation and googled *Location of Minotaur murders*. A map of England appeared showing twelve red circles. Using a pen and notepad scavenged from the hotel he sketched an approximation of the image. Then he joined the dots in the order of each murder. He unfolded his drawing of Minotaur's maze and smoothed out the creases.

When viewed side by side, the route through the labyrinth was roughly the same shape as the lines connecting the location of each murder. The town in which victim number one was killed marked the entrance. The location of victim number two denoted the first branching pathway. Each subsequent victim, including Zoe, marked turning points along the route to the centre. Minotaur needed to claim just one more soul to reach the middle. If David's theory was correct, the next murder – and end point – would take place in a town called Harwood.

Reducing the scope of his search should have felt like an achievement. But, with a population of fifty-five thousand, and covering an area of more than $150km^2$ it was difficult to feel overly confident. There was also no way to predict when the thirteenth attack might occur.

David spent the next hour scouring a Google map of Harwood. It was a patience-testing task that did nothing to ease his throbbing head. But then he saw it – two words in the north-west part of town.

Shadwell Estate.

Was it possible that an area with that name might be referred to locally as 'The Shades'? It was tenuous – desperate even – and yet David could not shake the feeling he was onto something. He zoomed in to view that section of the map in more detail. Street names appeared, a railway station, schools, and several places of worship. He zoomed in again to reveal minor roads, a doctor's surgery, restaurants, a halal butcher, an MOT test centre and a tanning boutique.

David referred to the map he had drawn while exploring The Shades online. He had been ejected upon reaching the allotment, suggesting that area, more than any other, had significance. He angled the drawing, trying to match his scribbled lines to the on-screen geography. At first glance there appeared to be nothing, even remotely close, in or around the Shadwell Estate.

Disheartened but not ready to give up, he repositioned the map, zoomed out to increase the area viewable on-screen, and glanced from one image to the other. He was suddenly struck by how similar they now appeared. Not just in terms of the general street layout, but there was also a children's play area and an allotment nearby. Sliding the mouse sideways, he positioned the cursor over Google Map's Pegman.

David grabbed the intrepid little explorer and dropped him into position for a more convenient street level view. The map reconstituted into a high definition panoramic photograph that could be rotated a full three hundred and sixty degrees. With a growing sense of déjà vu, David clicked the on-screen arrow and the image moved forward along the road. As he embarked on a virtual tour of the Shadwell Estate, he tracked progress against his own map.

What if this trail of breadcrumbs really did lead to Minotaur? Assuming he could capture and restrain him, it was unlikely the killer would reveal anything of value unless properly motivated. David would need Frank's assistance to design and craft a suitably persuasive torture device. The image of a scold's bridle formed in his mind. A cage, barely large enough to contain a human head, with steel rods positioned across the brow and at each temple to be tightened as and when required.

David felt the gorge rise. *Is this who I am now?*

If he followed this path there was a chance – however remote – that he might one day be reunited with his son. But in doing so, would Charlie even recognise the man his father had become? And what about Frank? He was already facing an assault charge and the possibility of a custodial sentence. If his father-in-law were to be implicated and found guilty, he was likely to spend the rest of his days in prison.

As David clicked left, shifting his view to another road lined with semi-detached houses, the déjà vu intensified. In front of him was an old-fashioned telephone box, identical to the one he had seen in Other Life. Telegraph poles, power lines, and drainage covers, all in the same position. There was no doubt about it. This was the street to which the Cody avatar had teleported.

Claremont Road.

And yet for all its familiarity, there were notable differences. The Other Life version must have been based on how the area looked twenty or thirty years ago. The boxy houses had been upgraded. Hedges uprooted and replaced with iron-rail fencing. Front lawns dug up and paved over. Only number 29, with its messy thatch of wisteria trailing over the porch, was the same.

CHAPTER THIRTY-EIGHT

Christopher Wynn had always felt like an outsider. Over time, he came to understand his purpose in the world. But to fulfil that role he had to adapt. To pass unnoticed through what was laughably called 'civilised society', it was necessary to blend in. He had sat on park benches and in coffee shops, observing the comings and goings of so-called 'ordinary' people.

Rich or poor, happy or sad, so much of what they had to say was pointless. Facile platitudes, idle gossip, and irrelevant chit-chat. These directionless meat-bags conjured the illusion of normality while harbouring the darkest of secrets. Resentment, bitterness, jealousy, rage, lust, and deviancy. They were hypocrites, suppressed by their own true nature. They buried their natural instincts while posting fake smiles on social media.

In cataloguing these behaviours Wynn made an interesting discovery. Those who projected an appropriate level of confidence were rarely challenged. The default reaction tended to be respect, or even submission. It was how he had so effortlessly slipped into the guise of Paul Dawson – a loving son who visited his mother at the Greenacres Residential Care Home.

"If you ask me," he said, "the council need to get their act together, and fast. There are potholes all the way along the street and it's only getting worse. One of these days there's going to be a nasty accident."

Alice's brittle fingers continued to scratch the fabric of her chair, sending spongy particles onto the carpet.

As Wynn ran through his usual list of silence-filling small talk, he surveyed the day room. A couple of unfamiliar faces had appeared since his last visit. A man in his nineties with hollow cheeks and thick-lensed glasses watched some banal gameshow. The other new arrival was a tiny Jamaican woman who looked to be away with the fairies. Both would have transferred from a hospital or sheltered accommodation to join the frail, the infirm and the incontinent.

Wynn despised them all. Their sunken eyes, their vein-mottled skin and their weakness. He would have gladly killed them all with a house brick. Shattering their feeble skulls like so many goose eggs.

"Hello, Mr Dawson."

Wynn flashed Kim a smile. "Please, call me Paul." His words sounded innocent enough, but he made a point of locking eyes with the woman who would be his final victim.

"Are you Paul?" said Alice, her brow creasing.

"Yes, Mum."

"But you live in Canada with Olivia and the children."

"No, Mum. I'm right here."

"Oh. I thought..." Alice's moment of clarity was gone. Her eyes lost focus and the sentence was left hanging.

Kim finished her shift just after 6pm. It would have been earlier, but Mr Frederickson had another of his accidents. One change of bedding later and she was finally done for the day. She said her goodbyes and retrieved her bike. The evening was colder than expected. Zipping her fleece she braced herself for a chilly ride home. As she unfolded her bike her thoughts turned to Paul Dawson.

He was just so... She paused, searching for the right word. Charming? Intriguing? Alluring? By the time she put foot to pedal she was no closer to finding a suitable adjective. Pushing away, she followed a graceful arc onto the road. The chill dispelled her weariness and as she picked up speed further synonyms sprang to mind. Beguiling... Captivating... Enticing...

Stop it, she chided herself. *You're not some lovestruck teenager!*

Bewitching... Tempting... Seductive...

A romantic at heart, Kim fell in love easily, and always ended up getting hurt. But Paul seemed like a genuinely nice man. He was well-mannered, loved his mum, and was handsome in his own unassuming way. These moments of ill-judged fantasy opened the floodgates to her many long-standing hang-ups.

She was no spring chicken by any stretch of the imagination. Despite cycling to and from work her hips remained stubbornly wide and her belly annoyingly soft. Her buttocks were flabby, and cellulite dimpled the backs of her legs. And, to top it all, her breasts – which had always been her best feature – were losing their fight against gravity.

"You are really pretty."

Those had been Paul's words only a few days previously. The comment had been followed by a hasty apology and the moment was gone. If only she had the kind of ballsy attitude some of her more confident friends enjoyed. Then, maybe, she might have done something other than flush red and stammer like an idiot.

By the time Kim was back in her flat, her bike folded and stashed in the hallway, she was chilled to the bone. Even with the heating on full blast she had to snuggle into her fluffiest onesie to get warm. As she stood in the kitchenette, waiting for a microwavable lasagne to ping, she glanced outside. Across the road, beyond a line of beech trees, the allotments were barely visible in the fading light.

It was cold and gloomy in the potting shed. Its single window was no longer covered by old newspaper. Instead, the glass had been sprayed with black paint. With the door bolted from the inside, Wynn's privacy was assured. He sat on the same rusty picnic chair he had sat on as a child.

The laptop balanced on his knees showed a live video stream from the cameras hidden around Kim's apartment. A high-angled image showed her spooning red-and-yellow slop onto her plate. She plucked a knife and fork from the cutlery drawer and moved away from the camera's field of vision. She appeared in another portion of the screen, sat down at her tiny dining table, and thumbed a TV remote.

The lasagne was stodgy and tasteless, so Kim ended up scraping the last few mouthfuls into the bin. Her eyelids were heavy, and the soap opera she had been watching was little more than background noise.

After pouring herself a large glass of red wine, she found a packet of tealight candles and headed for the bathroom. Kim had opted for a nautical theme, with navy-blue walls and shiny, white floor tiles. The mirror's frame resembled the helm of a ship. A half roll of toilet paper hung from a loop of mooring rope. On the windowsill was a ceramic dolphin, a wooden anchor, and a conch shell.

Setting down her glass, she lit the candles, set the hot and cold taps running and adjusted their temperature. She dropped in an ethically sourced bath bomb and watched the mountain of colourful suds take shape.

The camera had been placed deep within the conch shell, but its lens was prone to misting from increased humidity. As far as Wynn was concerned, that moment could not come soon enough.

He gagged at the sight of the woman's heavy breasts which threatened to spill from her flesh-toned bra. She undid the high-mounted clasp and pulled the undergarment aside. Wynn screwed his eyes shut, knowing he would be sick on the spot if he caught sight of those sagging mounds.

When he looked again, Kim had settled into the quivering foam. She reached for her wine and took a contented sip. He knew how this scene would play out, and it involved much shuddering and moaning. Kim was at her sexual peak in the days leading up to her period.

Wynn had not needed to pick through her bin bags to confirm this detail. It was all there in her diary. With this routine established, his next move was clear.

CHAPTER THIRTY-NINE

William Merriweather blew on his tea, sending a gentle ripple across its surface. In all their years of marriage Iris had yet to make him a decent brew. The beverage was at least three shades too dark for his liking, and far too hot. It was almost as if she were doing it on purpose as part of some domestic war of attrition.

He could have gone to the kitchen and added an extra splash of milk but refused to do so on principle. Besides, he did not want to be told off for deserting his post. William was under strict instructions to look out for David. Under no circumstances was he to go sneaking off to read the newspaper. He peered through the net curtains and was relieved to see a taxi pulling up outside. "This could be him. Yes... it's him."

Iris bustled out of the kitchen and opened the door before David had a chance to knock. "Hi," he said with a smile that soon faded. "Is everything all right?"

Taking his second cab ride of the day, David went straight to the hospital. The last time he had walked those sterile corridors had been with Zoe for her twelve-week scan. They had practically floated out of the examination room, their eyes fixed on the ultrasound printout. This time, the whole place seemed claustrophobic and so much darker. He made his way to the cardiac care unit in a daze. How could this have happened to Frank of all people?

"Mr Knight?"

David turned to see Detective Sergeant Vikram Prakesh. The young detective looked shaken. His hair, usually so neatly combed, fell in loose strands over his face. "Please, sit down."

Prakesh explained that paramedics had arrived within minutes but downplayed his own role in saving Frank's life. He then introduced David to Doctor Fanning. A tall cardiologist with twinkling eyes and a neat goatee.

Fanning's tone was matter of fact. "Your father-in-law suffered a heart attack. It was brought on by a ruptured cholesterol deposit which triggered a blood clot. We were able to dissolve the clot and he's responding well. There's unlikely to be any permanent damage but he'll have to make some changes to his lifestyle. He'll need to eat sensibly, exercise regularly and above all, avoid unnecessary stress."

"Can I see him?"

"Yes, of course. Come with me."

David followed the doctor to a side room. Frank lay in bed, hooked up to an intravenous drip and a machine that measured his heart rate, blood pressure and oxygen levels. A nasal cannula was clipped to his septum. Its translucent pipe snaked across the bed sheet and into the wall. "Frank? It's me, David."

Frank's heavy-lidded eyes opened, and he managed a small nod of recognition.

"He's been through a lot," said the doctor, "so no more than five minutes, all right?"

David nodded. "Thank you."

Prakesh and Fanning exited the room and closed the door. David stared at Frank's ghost-white face. His father-in-law attempted to say something but winced from the effort.

"Don't speak."

"Did you... find him?" Frank's words were as dry as sand.

"Let's not talk about that right now. You need to rest."

Frank's face was resolute. "Did you... find him?"

"I don't know," David said with a sigh. "Maybe. I've got a lead."

"You have to... finish it."

"No. I'm turning everything over to the police. I'll do it anonymously. We won't be implicated in what happened to Jenrick."

"He's... dead."

Those two words smashed David in the face with the force of a mule's kick. "Did you...?"

"I... went back–"

"Jesus, Frank! What were you thinking?"

"He was... already dead."

"Suicide?"

Frank's reply was a small nod.

David began pacing the floor. "There will be bruises and burns. They'll know there's more to it. Shit!"

The door swung open and a nurse with a stern expression hurried into the room. Plucking a clipboard from the end of Frank's bed she checked his vital signs.

"How are you feeling, Mr Crocker?"

Frank gave her a weary thumbs up.

"Do you need anything?"

Frank shook his head.

"Right then," she said, turning to David, "I'll have to ask you to leave now. Mr Crocker needs to rest."

"Two more minutes. Please."

The nurse thawed a little. "Two minutes, but not a second more."

When they were alone again David returned to Frank's bedside. "What happened?"

"He saw me.... The detective... I should have... fronted it out... but I ran. Stupid... So stupid." He closed his eyes, taking several deep breaths before attempting to speak again. "You have to... kill... Minotaur."

"Frank... No... Don't ask me to–"

"You have to... finish... it."

The door swung open, and the nurse bustled back in. "Come on, time to go."

David was ushered from the room to find Prakesh waiting in the corridor. He had been joined by Rybak. In her bright-blue duffle coat, she reminded David of Paddington Bear. "How is he?" she asked.

"Tired."

"I'm not surprised. Mr Crocker has had a busy day."

"Meaning?"

"Why don't you let me buy you a coffee and we can–"

"Maybe another time."

"Another time is likely to involve a more formal request."

Frank's words popped into David's head. *I should have... fronted it out.* With so few options available, it was worth a try. "You might want to think about securing legal representation for your colleague here."

Both Prakesh and Rybak looked sideswiped by the audacity of this comment.

"I'm sorry?" The detective inspector's voice struck a note somewhere between laughter and indignation.

"Don't you think my father-in-law has been through enough? The last thing he needs is to be chased by you lot. Now look what's happened. He could die!"

"The doctor said–"

"I don't care what the bloody doctor said. I'll be speaking to my solicitor about this." David pushed past the detectives on his way to the lobby where a lift was waiting and jabbed the ground-floor button. As the doors slid shut a slender pair of hands appeared in the gap and forced them apart.

"A word of advice, Mr Knight," said Rybak. "For your son's sake, think long and hard about what you do next."

David said nothing. Her words just fuelled his rage. Eventually she let her hands fall away and the doors slid shut with a clunk. David's mind was filled with dark thoughts as he left the hospital. Anyone approaching had no choice but to veer out of his way. He was oblivious to their tuts and muttered obscenities.

Even with Frank's help, the odds of finding Charlie and killing Minotaur would have been long. With his father-in-law laid up in hospital, they stretched way off into the horizon. Nevertheless, David kept returning to the same, inescapable truth; the police were useless. He had experienced their lack of progress and bad judgement first-hand. Their ineptitude had been laid bare at every stage of the investigation and the media continued to berate them daily. If he were to pass on everything he had discovered, would they even bother to look at it?

A dozen or so patients and visitors had congregated outside the main doors. Most were on their phones while sucking vape pods. David barrelled through the berry-scented smog and stepped off the kerb, directly in front of a white Kuga. The driver slammed on the brakes bringing the vehicle to a screeching halt. "Look where you're going, you idiot!" called the driver, an obese man with piggy eyes.

David looked right through him.

"Get out of the way!" The driver gestured furiously for David to move.

David stepped back to the kerb, allowing the furious man to resume his journey. In some alternate reality, he would have been catapulted over the bonnet to be left with concussion and a broken arm. In another reality, Zoe and Charlie were alive and safe.

Rybak plucked a plastic cup from a dispenser and filled it with water from the cooler. She returned to the seating area outside the cardiac care unit and handed Prakesh the drink.

"Thanks," he said, taking a sip.

"Are you all right?"

"Yes, Guv."

"I think you should go home and get some rest."

"I'm fine. Really."

"You saved a man's life today. That's not nothing."

"If it weren't for me, it wouldn't have happened in the first place."

"What is it I'm always telling you?"

"Go with my gut instinct."

"And is that what you did back there?"

"Yes, Guv."

"Well, there you are then."

"He could have just been out for a walk."

"Come on, Vik, you don't believe that any more than I do. Besides, innocent people don't tend to run when they see a copper."

"Even so—"

"Even so, nothing. Let's just wait and see what they get from

Jenrick's security footage and that baseball bat you found. This time tomorrow we might have enough to–"

She was cut short by an insistent chime. Digging out her phone she took what turned out to be a brief and one-sided exchange.

Prakesh watched expectantly as Rybak gathered her thoughts. "Guv...?"

"That was Loveday. They've found the Subaru."

CHAPTER FORTY

The Carlton Bridge railway station was a twenty-minute walk along a road that had, over the years, claimed several lives. Long-dead bouquets were tied to lamp posts at irregular intervals. A constant stream of traffic flashed by as David trekked along the grass verge.

At the halfway point was a DIY megastore. The vast retail outlet offered an immense range of products. Aisle after aisle of everything anyone could possibly need to fix, improve, or expand their home and garden. Customers and tradesmen trawled the shelves and displays. Loading up baskets and trolleys with hardware, tools, and assorted supplies. David rarely visited places like this. Anything that involved being green-fingered or handy around the house had always been Zoe's department.

He made his way past displays of hot tubs, barbecues, and lawnmowers, through the interior lighting section and past the wallpapers, paints, tiles, and laminate flooring. The tools section did not disappoint. David scanned an impressive array of cordless drills, circular saws, and nail guns.

Their pros were obvious. Each device would make short

work of skin, bone, muscle, and sinew. They would inflict untold pain and irreparable damage. They were sturdy, well-made, and came with a three-year guarantee. But these devices were heavy, not easy to conceal and most required both hands to operate.

David moved along the aisle and found a sixteen-ounce claw hammer and a twenty-eight-ounce hatchet. Both items had a carbon steel head fitted to a wooden handle. Similar products had fibreglass handles with soft rubber grips but there was something reassuring about the feel of hickory. Next, he selected a pair of needle-point pliers with a sturdy side cutter. The store did not sell hunting knives, so he opted instead for a standard trimming knife with a quick-slide retractable blade.

A bag, he thought. *I need a bag.*

CHAPTER FORTY-ONE

Black mould had claimed the bathroom. It was in the grouting between the tiles, the sealant around the tub, and along the shower curtain's ragged edges. The ceiling was particularly bad. What had begun as a few dark speckles here and there had spread, mottling every inch of paintwork. Such things did not concern Wynn. The bathroom was a place for him to clean and relieve himself. Nothing more.

He had used clippers to shave his head, then a disposable razor to scrape away the residue. The hour-long process had left him with a gleaming scalp. Raw in places. Bloody in others.

During his most recent trip to the supermarket, he had purchased supplies for the next six weeks of self-imposed quarantine. Food, drink, and vital nutrients to sustain him while his hair grew back.

When fleeing the crime scene there was always a chance he would be spotted, and his hairless description relayed to the authorities. Anyone buying multiple tubes of hair removal cream from the same retailer would immediately attract suspicion. It was for that reason he sourced the depilatory lotion from a range of different pharmacies.

His pubic region alone required the contents of one whole tube. Most of his body was covered in a downy fluff, but the dense thatch between his legs was like wire wool by comparison. He massaged the rose-scented lotion into his groin and inner thighs. Moving onto his belly and chest, arms, and legs, he smeared the cream over himself until all but one tube was squeezed flat. He applied the last of it to the stubble covering his cheeks and chin before shifting focus to his eyebrows and lashes.

The product was meant to be washed away three minutes after application. Counting away the seconds, Wynn slammed the louver above the bathroom's frosted window shut. With nowhere to go the steam drifted around the room in lazy swirls. He watched condensation form and trickle down the tiles. At what he estimated to be the halfway point he twisted the taps anti-clockwise. Water gushed from the twin taps into the bath. Wynn flicked a switch diverting the flow to the shower head. The action triggered the sound of clanking and groaning from somewhere deep within the house.

Anyone unfamiliar with 29 Claremont Road would have called a plumber. But the ancient pipework had been making that same racket since Wynn was a boy. The noise did not bother him, it was the memories it stirred. Unwanted, hateful memories. They churned and writhed like dark beasts wallowing in some netherworld swamp.

"I'll have a look at the weekend," his father had once said of the clamorous water system. That was his stock response to most things. The truth was, his dad had never got around to looking at anything, with the notable exception of his slut. His father's betrayal had set the dominoes falling. In marrying Alan, Daphne Wynn had filled the hole in her heart with a malignant tumour.

Wynn stepped into the bath, angling the shower head so the water sprayed onto his chest. The pressure, although sluggish, was enough to cleave the hair from his skin. He watched it part company with his body and slither away down the plughole. Dragging fingers across his limbs he felt little resistance as the rest of the hair slithered away. The depilatory cream stunk to high heaven but worked wonders. The lightest of strokes across his stomach opened a track of virgin flesh. His hands moved between his legs dislodging coarse thickets of pubic hair.

For Wynn, this epilation was more about transformation than mere cleansing. Like a butterfly emerging from its chrysalis, or a snake shedding its skin. It was through this ritual that Christopher Wynn became Minotaur.

Beyond the sound of running water, the hollow clang of ancient plumbing continued, calling to mind another sound from his childhood.

CHAPTER FORTY-TWO

1978

Clank! Clank! Clank!

It was the bedpost in his mother's room knocking against the wall. Young Christopher Wynn heard it most nights. He curled up under the cotton sheets and winter blanket, knees tucked up to his chin and hands clamped over his ears.

Clank! Clank! Clank!

"Shut up!" he whimpered. "Shut up! Shut up! Shut up!"

Clank! Clank! Clank!

Christopher pushed his index fingers deep into his ears until pain flared in the delicate canals.

Clank! Clank! Clank!

Since the abuse began, Christopher rarely managed more than a few hours' sleep each night. Kids at school called him 'The Zombie' because of his sunken eyes and gaunt features.

Clank! Clank! Clank!

He threw aside the bedding and padded over to the door. Turning its knob as quietly as possible he tiptoed along the landing.

Clank! Clank! Clank!

As he approached his mother's bedroom, he heard a low and raspy grunt.

"Urh! Urh! Urh!"

On and on it went. A grim cacophony.

Clank! Clank! Clank!

"Urh! Urh! Urh!"

Christopher opened the door just enough to see what was going on. The moon's glow illuminated Alan's bony rear end as it bobbed up and down. He lay on top of Daphne, hands clamped around her wrists as he thrust into her.

Clank! Clank! Clank!

"Urh! Urh! Urh!"

The boy watched in silence, wanting to heave from the sour funk that filled the room. Alan grabbed Daphne's plump breasts and began kneading them like bread dough.

"No..." she moaned, in obvious discomfort. Alan lowered his mouth and bit down hard.

"No!" she cried again, louder this time. "I don't like it. Stop."

Alan continued pawing and sucking as he rammed into her, again and again.

"Alan! Please! No!"

Christopher ran to the bed and grabbed Alan's sandy locks with both hands. He pulled with every ounce of strength his little body could muster.

"Get off my mum!"

Alan slid free and landed with a high-pitched "Oof" on the floor. Daphne sat up, covering herself with the blanket.

"You little bastard!" shrieked the naked man. His semi-erect member flapped around like a pale eel as he writhed on the carpet.

The boy ran to his mother, arms opening for a hug. "Are you all right, Mum?"

"Christopher..." she said, in a faraway voice. "What have you done?"

"He was hurting you."

"No... he was just... oh no..."

Shuffling out of bed, she pushed Christopher aside to check on Alan. "Are you all right, my darling?"

"No, I'm not! He could have crippled me!"

"Mum, he's not who you think he is."

"What are you talking about, child?"

"He's a bad man."

"Chrissy...?" Alan's voice was loaded with menace.

Words that had been trapped inside Christopher for months came spilling out. "When we go to the shed, he puts his thing in my mouth. It's horrible. He wees out all this white stuff and I don't like it. Make him stop, Mum. Please make him stop."

"Liar!" Alan jabbed one of his long fingers at the boy. "You're a dirty liar!"

"It's true. I wouldn't lie. I promise. He makes me do it every time we go there. I hate it and I hate him. I wish he would go away and leave us alone forever."

Daphne was trembling. Her mouth a thin slit as her lips curled inwards.

"You don't believe him, do you? Baby, you know I would never do anything like that."

"He did! Cross my heart and hope to die. He said you wouldn't do it, so it had to be me. He said he'd hurt you if I didn't, or if I told anyone."

"You're evil! There's no other word for it. Telling horrible lies about me. Stop it. Stop it right now." He hauled himself up off the floor and clutched his genitals. A ghastly attempt at preserving his modesty.

Christopher put his hands out to his mother, desperate to feel her arms fold around him. "Mum?"

Daphne remained still, struggling to understand what she had just heard.

"You need to have a word with this kid of yours. If you don't, he'll be trouble. Mark my words."

Then it happened. Almost as if a switch had been flicked. Daphne's expression morphed from vacant to wild-eyed fury. The sheet fell away as she grabbed her son and unleashed a torrent of blows, smacking him around the head, back, arms and shoulders. The boy tried to shield himself, but his thin arms offered little in the way of protection.

"You horrible disgusting child!" Each word was emphasised with another stinging slap.

"Mum, no... please..."

"How dare you say that about your father! How dare you!"

"He's not my–"

"Be quiet! I don't want to hear another word out of your filthy mouth. You horrid boy!"

Christopher did not see the next blow coming. Her right hand connected with the left side of his face with such force that his head whipped sideways. The pain was excruciating, as if his cheek was on fire. She grabbed his ear between thumb and forefinger and dragged him from the room. The last thing he saw was Alan, a vicious grin on his face as he pulled up his Y-fronts.

Christopher had never seen his mother so angry. She practically threw him into the bathroom. With a tug of the light cord, her nakedness was illuminated in all its pasty-white glory. Her slack belly resembled a mound of slowly melting ice cream. The puckered flesh spilled over an untamed mass of pubic hair. Her pendulous breasts hung inches from Christopher's terrified face. A network of pale veins were prominent under the skin. Her dark bulging nipples were distended like a pair of upturned sink plungers. The right one still bore signs of Alan's recent attention – red raw from teeth marks and burst blood vessels. "Open your mouth!"

Christopher shook his head vehemently, determined not to allow whatever punishment she had in mind to happen.

"Let me help with that," said Alan, as if he were offering to take out the bins. He took a firm hold of Christopher's face and wrenched his jaws apart. The boy's arms circled frantically as he tried to pull himself free.

His mother picked up a tablet of toffee-yellow soap from the basin. There was a moment when she hesitated, as if racked by second thoughts but the reprieve was short-lived. She pushed the soap into Christopher's mouth and scrubbed.

CHAPTER FORTY-THREE

The journey was scheduled to take around three hours and involve two trains and a cab ride. Assuming there were no delays, David would arrive in Harwood by 5pm. He sat next to a quirkily-dressed woman who had a choppy hairstyle and multiple piercings. Her perfume was familiar. Sweet and floral, but not overpowering. David recognised it as a favourite of Zoe's. He closed his eyes and with that scent in his nostrils, it was like she was there with him – sitting by his side, as the train rattled along.

When he opened his eyes, he saw rolling hills and patchwork fields. The glass soon became foggy from his breath. He watched the misty patch shrink from its outer edges to its central point until it was gone. He breathed on it again and with the tip of his finger, wrote, *Darrian Hestead.*

Again, the mist faded, and the name vanished. David expelled another couple of shallow breaths as he puzzled over its meaning. Minotaur was obsessed with his maze. Was it such a leap to think he might also have a thing for anagrams? A clue to his identity could be hidden somewhere in those fourteen letters. It was just a matter of rearranging them into the correct order. But how many meaningful combinations could there be? Was it possible the killer's real name was jumbled up in there somewhere?

David mentally re-ordered the letters to form Ian, Ted, Thad, Dan, Stan, Adrian, and Ethan. That assumed the killer had a traditional Anglo-Saxon name. If not, then all bets were off. But serial killers tended to hunt within their own ethnic group. David recalled that Minotaur's victims had all been Caucasian females, so maybe the killer was indeed white. Exhaling a further breath, David studied the letters.

CHAPTER FORTY-FOUR

The chief forensics officer was a gruff Glaswegian named McKay. He had a flushed complexion, and eyes like bullets. His workshop resembled a mini aircraft hangar. Strip lighting suspended from trusses in the high ceiling bathed everything in white light. His team had disassembled the Subaru, examined, and referenced the parts, and laid them out across the shiny floor. Judging from their arrangement and spacing, McKay had an obsessive compulsive's eye for symmetry.

He stood with Rybak and Prakesh at a bank of monitors. The largest screen displayed a super-enhanced image of a tyre tread. Narrow grooves embedded with dirt filled the screen. Along its left-hand side were thumbnail pictures of the vehicle, its engine parts, chassis, and assorted components. Each had its own filename and story to tell.

McKay removed his glasses and inspected them for smears. Taking a microfibre cloth from his shirt pocket he set to work polishing them as he spoke. His Merchant City accent had an undeniable musical quality. "Uniform discovered it during a search of storage units on the Oak Road industrial estate. That's a quarter mile outside the original parameters so it was only recently flagged for a visit. The vehicle was found in a lock-up registered to a 'Darrian Hestead'. We ran it through our system but drew a blank. The car was reported stolen two months ago and fitted with plates from another vehicle."

Rybak sighed, although her expectations had not been high. "I suppose it's too much to hope CCTV picked something up."

"The nearest camera has been out of action since last Easter."

Rybak gestured to the monitor. "So, what exactly are we looking at here?"

Having finished cleaning his glasses, McKay slipped them back into position. He plucked a pencil from the desk and used it to indicate the on-screen image. "To start with we have traces of tricalcium silicate, dicalcium silicate, and tetracalcium aluminoferrite. Then there's sodium oxide, potassium oxide and just for good measure, a side order of gypsum."

Rybak seized on what appeared to be a slight pause to interject. "Can we pretend for a moment, that I failed GCSE chemistry?"

McKay feigned surprise. "Oh, I'm sorry. I thought you wanted it exactly. In that case, let's call it what it is; concrete."

"Concrete?"

"Most likely from debris that's more than fifty years old. Now, you might be wondering, what's so significant about this sample? Nothing in and of itself, but it's the blend of other substances that's interesting. There's clay, sand, and limestone for a start, although again, hardly what you might call unique. But then we have trace elements of tetrafluoromethane, propylene glycol and dimethyl ether. The type of chemical compounds typically found in–"

"Aerosol spray paint."

McKay arched an eyebrow as he turned to Prakesh. "Do I detect a misspent childhood?"

"Uh..."

The hint of a smile cracked McKay's dour features. "But yes, judging from the chemical compounds, I would say it's residue from solvent-based aerosol spray paint."

"The old mill." There was no trace of doubt in Prakesh's tone. "I was over there a few years ago when I was in uniform. A bunch of druggies beat up a homeless man."

Rybak nodded. "I remember. Nasty business."

"The whole place is covered in graffiti. There are empty paint cans everywhere."

"And like the lock-up it would have fallen outside of the original search parameters. Did you find anything else?"

"Yes." McKay's features hardened. "There is something."

Rybak knew that look only too well. She had seen it on the faces of countless scene-of-crime officers and pathologists over the years.

"The vehicle's interior has been scrubbed with bleach. We didn't find any hair or fibre so it's likely it was also given a going over with a vacuum cleaner." McKay paused to call up another image on the screen. This time it was a picture of the velour mat from the Subaru's boot. "This material is five-millimetre thick, Polypropelene. It isn't waterproof so rather than settle on the surface a liquid will soak into the material. As you can see, it's black so unless you were to specifically look for a damp patch it would be almost impossible to spot."

"What did you find?"

"Urine. The lining is stained with urine."

CHAPTER FORTY-FIVE

David awoke to an incessant chikka-chikka beat. The woman with an abundance of nose rings, earrings and lip rings was listening to music through earbuds. Shaking off the last remnants of sleep, David checked his watch. Harwood was fifteen minutes away. His view of the world had changed from sweeping countryside to dingy side streets and overgrown back gardens.

He had dozed off while attempting to unscramble the anagram. Given Minotaur's obsession with the maze, it seemed likely there would be some connection to the same Greek myth.

Theseus had entered the labyrinth and slain the Minotaur but there was more to the story than that. Daedalus designed the maze to be impossible to navigate. Its corridors were said to be littered with the bones of foolhardy explorers. They died, alone in the dark, of starvation, madness or torn apart by its horned denizen. Ariadne, daughter of King Minos, had gifted Theseus a ball of thread which he unrolled as he ventured deeper into the maze. Upon killing the Minotaur, he retraced his steps by following the thread.

Ariadne's Thread.

David mentally ticked off the letters a second and third time, but there was no doubt about it. Darrian Hestead was an anagram of Ariadne's Thread. But rather than a ball of twine, the killer's trail consisted of twelve women and an unborn child. The name was not intended to be a clue to Minotaur's identity. It was a sick joke to taunt his pursuers and further twist the knife.

CHAPTER FORTY-SIX

For as long as he could remember, Vikram Prakesh had been a disappointment to his family. Not so much his mother. She had always been loving, supportive and quietly progressive in her values. His father and two older brothers were a different story. They were doctors, and highly respected in their chosen field of expertise. Prakesh had quit medical school during his first year. That was bad enough but announcing his intention to join the police shook the family to its core.

For a while he was not certain he would be welcomed home again. His mother, ever the peacemaker, had been the one to bring them back together. Criticism of his chosen career was forbidden, especially around the dinner table. It prompted his father and brothers to switch strategy. Rather than outright rebukes, their methods of belittling him became more insidious.

"Are you looking for a transfer to the city?" It sounded like a casual enough inquiry but in their minds, Carlton Bridge was a sleepy backwater and therefore a waste of his time and talent.

"When will you be promoted?" was another all-too frequent question.

"Chief Superintendent Prakesh has a nice ring to it," his father had said.

"Chief Constable Prakesh sounds better," countered his eldest brother.

The subtext was clear. If he was intent on bucking family tradition in favour of becoming a copper, then he had better ensure he was a bloody good one.

When he and Rybak joined the Minotaur investigation, Prakesh had naively thought they would make a difference. But McKay's grim revelation had brought their lack of progress into sharp focus.

Prakesh glanced skywards as he drove and saw ominous, slate-grey clouds. It would be touch and go whether they reached the mill before it started to rain.

"Why would he take the boy?" It was a question that had been bothering Rybak since that fateful night. "It's such a risk, and so out of character. His violence has always been directed squarely towards women. Specifically, middle-aged white women. There must be a reason he took such an abrupt left turn."

"Maybe something in his life has changed."

"Maybe. Or maybe it's a statement. 'Look at me. I can do whatever I want and there's not a damn thing anyone can do about it'."

"None of the murders have been sexually motivated. He just doesn't fit the profile of a pederast."

"He's not. A fledgling child killer perhaps but I don't see him getting his kicks from molesting the poor little blighter."

"What if Charlie's abduction has nothing to do with sex, or even the act of killing. What if…?" Prakesh paused, trying to marshal his thoughts. "What if he needs the boy?"

"What do you mean, 'needs'? Like as a companion? Or friend?"

"I wish I did. I mean, what if his plan all along was to sell the boy?"

Rybak shuddered at the thought. The prospect of someone evil enough to purchase a child from a serial killer sent ice water sluicing through her veins.

CHAPTER FORTY-SEVEN

The Audi crunched through gravel as it rolled through the mill's entrance. A heavy iron gate lay on the ground, consumed by a tangle of bracken. The other gate had been pulled aside allowing access to the abandoned grain silos.

Rybak flicked up the hood of her duffle coat as she stepped from the vehicle. Spots of rain were dotting the ground and the air held a promise of more to follow. Prakesh buttoned his jacket while scanning the dirt and debris. There was no shortage of sand and concrete beneath his feet. Probably some clay as well if he were to go looking for it.

The detectives walked side by side into what had once been a hive of industry but now resembled an apocalyptic film set. A jungle of weeds and wildflowers sprouted from cracks in the concrete. Charred remnants of wooden pallets and timber slats marked the spots where bonfires had been lit.

There was more graffiti than Prakesh remembered. Almost every square inch of exposed brickwork had been tagged or scribbled on. Judging from the array of complex and colourful pieces, the location was visited by serious artists as well as the usual delinquents. It was like a slowly decaying gallery of urban artwork. The tools of the trade were everywhere. Trays, rollers, and depleted aerosol cans. Prakesh could not help but admire the artistry around him.

Rybak was less enamoured with her surroundings. "It's off the beaten track but why come here? There's only one way in and one way out. Surely it would only make sense if this had been where he switched cars."

"Maybe he met someone. Maybe this is where he arranged to hand over the boy."

"Let's find out who owns the land. We'll get a team in to do a... full... grid... search..." Rybak's words trailed away but her eyes flicked from side to side.

"Guv?"

"We're being watched."

"Are you sure?"

"Positive."

"It could be Jamie."

"Jamie Hyde? The homeless man?"

Prakesh nodded. Turning slowly, he raised his hands in what he hoped looked to be a placating gesture. The rain was pitter-pattering and the wind beginning to pick up. He scanned the area but there were no obvious signs of life beyond a few plump pigeons. The first of the three towering silos lay ahead, and the remains of an administration building were on the left. To the right was a loading bay that at some point had been repurposed as a rough and ready skateboard park.

"Jamie? My name is Vikram Prakesh. I'm a police officer. Do you remember I spoke to you a few years ago? I took your statement after the attack." He paused, but his only response was the sound of wind and rain. "You're not in any trouble. We only want to ask you a few questions."

"Who's she?"

Prakesh glanced around, trying to pinpoint where the voice had come from.

"This is Maureen. She's police, like me."

"Is she your boss?"

"She is. We just want to ask you some questions. We're not here to cause you any problems. You have my word on that." His eyes flicked to the old building's open doorway. Its green paint peeled away to reveal the rotting woodwork. Inside, a few grubby floor tiles could be seen but beyond that lay an impenetrable gloom.

"Do you trust her?"

"Yes, Jamie. I trust her with my life."

This seemed to convince Jamie to leave the sanctuary of his hiding place. He shambled out of the tumbledown structure. The young man's thin frame was swamped by a filthy Parka jacket. A straggly beard framed a narrow face with sharp cheekbones.

"Thank you, Jamie," said Prakesh. "We really appreciate you talking to us."

Jamie didn't reply at first, he just watched Prakesh from the doorway. Grimy fingernails picked at the decaying paintwork. "Why did they do it? Those boys. Why did they hurt me?"

"I don't know. They were on drugs but that's no excuse. It was cowardly and despicable. I wish their sentences better reflected that."

"I remember you were nice to me."

"I wanted to help. I still do."

"But first you want me to answer your questions."

It was not a rebuke and yet Prakesh could not help but to take it as one. "A woman who lives a few miles from here was killed and her young son taken. We think whoever was responsible may have come here. They would have been driving a black car."

Jamie nodded. "I saw it."

Rybak walked forward but it was the wrong thing to do. Jamie retreated into the darkness so only the whites of his eyes could be seen.

"It's all right, Jamie." Rybak gave him an engaging smile. "I didn't mean to alarm you. Please, carry on."

Jamie stepped back into the light and looked her up and down. "I like your coat."

"Thank you. I like it too. What about you, Vik? Do you like it?"

"Um..."

Rybak smiled. "Vik doesn't like it. I don't think he likes any of my clothes. He's too polite to say anything, but I can tell. I am a detective after all. Most people think I dress like a crazy person, but you know what I say? Stuff them. I don't care what they think."

Apparently satisfied with her sincerity, Jamie approached them. "This way." He marched off towards the main gates, moving with ease through the broken glass and shattered breeze blocks. The detectives followed him to the middle of what had once been the forecourt.

"Here." Jamie pointed at his feet for emphasis. "They were standing right here."

"They?" Rybak's eyes narrowed. "You saw more than one person?"

"I saw two men. One man was in the black car. The other man was in a blue car."

"Can you describe them?"

Jamie turned to Prakesh. "The man in the black car was about your height. I didn't see his face because he was wearing a coat with a hood."

"Was he white? Black? Asian?"

"I think he was white."

"What about the other man?"

"He was white too, but much taller and fatter. He had long hair, down to here." Jamie indicated a point below his own shoulders.

"Did you see his face?"

"No. He was holding a big umbrella. It reminded me of sweeties my nanna used to buy. Raspberry bullseyes. Have you ever had a raspberry bullseye?"

"Yes," Rybak said. "My nanny always had a bag in the house. They're nice, aren't they?"

Jamie nodded, smiling as if recalling happier times.

"Is there anything else you can tell us about the men? Or their cars?"

"The blue car had a broken mirror on the..." Jamie paused to recall the detail, "driver's side. It was all wrapped up in tape."

"And where were you at the time?"

"In there." Jamie jabbed a finger at the derelict building. "I couldn't sleep. The roof leaks, so I was getting all wet. That's when I heard the black car."

"I don't suppose you can remember either of the registration numbers?"

"No. I'm sorry."

"What happened when the blue car arrived?"

Jamie's recollection on this point was surprisingly good. While not close enough to overhear the conversation, he was clear about the sequence of events, where the vehicles had been parked and where both men had been standing. "The big man with the umbrella was right there, where you are now." He indicated Prakesh. "And the hooded man was here, where I am. They talked for a while and then the hooded man took something out of his car and put it in the boot of the blue car."

"Jamie," Rybak said carefully, "do you have any idea what it might have been?"

Jamie parted his hands to indicate a length of approximately one metre. "It was all floppy, like a bag of clothes. The hooded man was about to go when he took something from his pocket and threw it to the big man. It bounced off his hand and landed..." Jamie glanced at the damp ground and pointed. "There."

Rybak took out her phone and thumbed on its torch. The cone of light illuminated concrete, loose stones, burgeoning weeds, and a flattened water bottle.

"You're being very helpful, Jamie. We're grateful, but is there anything else you can remember? Anything at all."

Jamie shook his head, looking genuinely sorry he could not be of more help.

"Vik?" said Rybak, pointing. "Do you see that? What does it look like to you?"

Only when Prakesh was close to ground level could he see what Rybak was looking at. Resting on its side amongst the shingle was the small blue plastic cap of an asthma inhaler.

CHAPTER FORTY-EIGHT

K im exchanged cheerful pleasantries with residents on her way through the day room. She held a cup of water in one hand and a paper ramekin containing Alice's medication in the other. It was approaching the end of another busy day, not helped by a colleague's unexpected absence. Kim had no reason to doubt the woman was unwell, but it meant more work for everyone else. "Alice? It's time for your... "

Alice's arms hung over the sides of her chair. Her limp fingers pointed at a dusting of sponge fragments on the carpet.

Kim remained at Greenacres until long after her shift had ended, sobbing quietly as the paramedics wheeled Alice away. The blanket covering her body seemed to lay flat on the gurney, as if the old lady was not even there. Tears were still flowing as Kim cycled home. It would be for the administrator to inform Alice's next of kin. The news would be broken in a sympathetic manner. Nevertheless, Kim had no doubt Paul would be devastated.

Minotaur checked his watch. Kim was never this late home, meaning one of the old bastards must have shat themselves or died. No cause for concern but it was stuffy and claustrophobic in the wardrobe. Sweat trickled down his back, armpits and between his legs. Flexing his limbs, he shifted his weight to keep the circulation flowing. As confined and uncomfortable as he felt, the hiding place had one distinct benefit. The clothes hanging around him bore Kim's essential fragrance. A combination of mid-range perfume, supermarket brand shampoo, fabric conditioner and her own uniquely feminine musk. If he closed his eyes, it was like she was there with him.

Kim steered her bike onto the kerb and freewheeled along the pavement until she reached her flat. Julius Ndogo smiled and waved at her. The Nigerian's huge muscles bulged under a black-and-white T-shirt bearing the Parental Advisory Explicit Content logo. The cuffs of his baggy skater jeans were rolled up over a pair of trainers that would have cost Kim her weekly salary. A plastic bag filled with choice delicacies from the local spicy chicken shop dangled from one hand. "Kim," he boomed, sliding his key into the lock. "You look so sad."

"I'm all right. Work stuff."

"You will come and join me for dinner, yes? Look, I have plenty." He held up his bag. It contained four polystyrene boxes and a two-litre bottle of cola. It was a sweet offer, but a Venn diagram of their food preferences would have consisted of two unconnected circles.

"That's very kind but I'm not hungry."

"If you change your mind, you know where I am."

Julius opened the front door and allowed Kim to wheel her bike in. They chatted a while longer. Light-hearted banter that went some way towards lifting her spirits.

They said goodbye and Julius thundered upstairs. Kim folded her bike and unlocked the door to her flat. She had a soft spot for the big man. He did not take himself seriously and had a kind heart – although what he was like with the unruly drunks at closing time was another matter. If it were not for his habit of playing rap songs with questionable lyrics at full volume, he would have been the perfect neighbour.

Her flat seemed quieter than usual. Gloomier and somehow foreboding.

Don't be ridiculous, she chided herself. There was nothing to be gained by projecting her own negative energy onto her surroundings. *Pull yourself together, you silly woman.*

Kim switched on a string of fairy lights, grabbed the remote and began channel hopping. In no mood for the usual soap opera histrionics, she settled on an early evening magazine show. The jovial hosts were chatting to an A-list movie star with a radiant smile about his new mega-budget action film.

Kim hung up her coat and kicked off her shoes, only half listening as the famous actor gushed about his director and co-stars. Kim had no interest in anything the multi-millionaire adrenaline junkie had to say. She just welcomed the temporary illusion of company.

Minotaur heard Kim moving around in the flat. Her thin carpets did nothing to dampen the sound of footsteps. He heard doors opening, muffled audio from the television and then the bedroom light clicked on. A sliver of illumination spilled through the crack between the wardrobe doors. She was undressing, he was sure of it. Probably getting ready for her bath.

A frisson ran through his body. Not at the thought of her nakedness but her proximity. The wardrobe door on the left-hand side swung open. Light flooded in but Minotaur did not flinch. He knew there was no chance of being seen from that angle. He was on the other side. Pressed as far into the corner as physics would allow and hidden by clothes. She pulled a dressing gown from its hanger, the door closed, and it was dark again. Minotaur adjusted the GoPro head strap, pulling it tight around his skull. Only when the camera was secure did he start recording.

CHAPTER FORTY-NINE

Kim tied the dressing gown belt in a loose knot as she strolled into the kitchenette. Removing a chrome stopper from a bottle of cheap wine she poured the last of it into a tumbler. The bottle remained upended until every drop had been drained.

The glamorous TV presenter drew her interview to a close and introduced an item about fly fishing. It was a clunking segue that left the A-list megastar looking bemused. Kim set a bath running and dropped in the last brightly coloured bomb from a fancy gift set. It frothed up into a mountain of bubbles, filling the room with a nose-prickling whiff of zesty avocado.

Kim studied her reflection as she sipped wine. She looked tired, haggard, and frumpy. Her next gulp emptied the glass. She closed her eyes, savouring the alcohol's warming effect. How could she have deluded herself that someone like Paul might be interested in her? It was the desperate fantasy of a pre-menopausal forty-something. When she opened her eyes, she saw the reflection of a bald man, watching her from the doorway. He was dressed in black and had something strapped to his head. The man's face, although hairless, was familiar.

Kim spun round as Minotaur swung the hammer. Instinctively raising an arm to shield herself, the steel head crunched into her radius bone, shattering it on impact. A gloved hand clamped over her mouth, cutting short her scream. The intruder shoved her into the wall, slamming her head against the tiles. "Shut up, bitch!"

As he raised the hammer to strike again, Kim smashed the tumbler into his cheek. There was a sharp crack as glass splintered. The intruder looked more shocked than hurt. Kim used this split-second advantage to shove the tumbler's broken edge deeper into his face, then rammed her knee into his groin. He yelped and bent double, releasing his grip just enough for her to pull away. As she bolted for the door, he grabbed the hem of her dressing gown. His grip was tight enough to yank her backwards, but only for a moment. Her fingers scrambled at the belt and pulled the knot free. The robe slid away, and she ran naked from the room.

"Help!" Kim shrieked. "Help! Help!"

She ran to the kitchenette, wrenched open the cutlery drawer and grabbed a meat knife with her good hand. The bald man charged at her, eyes blazing and blood streaming.

"Get away from me." She thrust the knife at him. "I'll kill you! I'll fucking kill you..." Her snarl was suddenly weakened by a flicker of recognition. "Paul...?"

Minotaur strode forward as if the meat knife was not even there.

Kim stabbed the intruder but instead of sinking into his chest the blade seemed to have no effect whatsoever. The man she knew as Paul Dawson brought the hammer down so hard it cracked her skull. She collapsed in a heap of naked flesh at his feet, twitched, and then lay still.

Minotaur had not expected her to fight back. Luckily for him, he always took the precaution of wearing a stab-proof vest.

The blade's impetus was absorbed by high-tensile Kevlar, dispersing the force amongst its synthetic fibre. He would be sore for a day or two, but serious injury had been averted.

There were sounds of movement from above. Minotaur's eyes darted to the ceiling, listening to the man-mountain in the flat upstairs. Footsteps, followed by a door opening and slamming shut. Then the clump-clump-clump of an eighteen-stone man hurrying downstairs. Minotaur rolled Kim onto her back and straddled her. The woman's large breasts hung limp on either side of her chest. She had a soft muffin-top belly and to his surprise her navel was pierced. Nothing fancy, just a little silver butterfly dangling from a ring.

The Nigerian neighbour was outside, yelling and banging at the door. "Kim? What's wrong?"

Ignoring the commotion, Minotaur slid the hunting knife free of its cowhide sheath.

"Kim? Are you all right in there?"

Minotaur stabbed the knife into the base of Kim's left breast. Blood pooled around the gleaming metal as he pushed deep into muscle and fat.

The door rattled in its frame from the frenzied hammering. "Kim!" called Julius. "Please open the door."

When the blade was hilt-deep, Minotaur grabbed the bloody gland and began to pull. He wrenched the knife left and right, widening the cut. This would not be pretty but would have to do. The breast peeled away with a squelch, leaving behind an oval-shaped flap of torn muscle.

Thunk! The Nigerian threw himself at the door with enough force to cause wood to splinter.

Thunk!

Minotaur made short work of removing the other breast. If the first part of this hideous mastectomy had been messy, the second was even more ragged. It did not matter. It would take more than shoddy knifework to spoil his legacy.

Thunk! Ragged cracks in the frame grew wider. The killer moved to the left of the door, so it would swing the other way when Julius broke through.

Thunk! Crack!

Metal twisted and wood split as the lock gave way. The door flew open, and there was Julius, shoulders heaving from the exertion. The first thing he saw was Kim, naked and butchered.

The knife struck with such force it severed the Nigerian's spinal cord between the third and fourth cervical vertebrae. He slumped to the carpet, face first, the last of his breath escaping in a series of erratic gurgles. Minotaur pulled the knife free, wiped the blade on the big man's shoulder, then returned it to the scabbard. There had been so much noise it was likely someone had called the police. He would need to move fast.

Locating a first aid kit, he used cotton wool and fabric plaster to patch his face up. Then he sloshed detergent around the floor and did what he could with a scrubbing brush to remove traces of his own blood.

Minotaur scooped up Kim's severed breasts and slid them into a ziplock freezer bag. He stashed the trophies in his rucksack, which left one final task. Grabbing a clump of hair, he dragged Kim's corpse into the bathroom as if it were cumbersome luggage.

When he released his grip the woman's head hit the tiles with a firm smack. Minotaur pressed his splayed fingers against her ragged chest wound. The glove's fabric made a slick scratchy sound as probing digits forced their way into the meat. When they were good and covered, he turned to the wall and swiped his index finger across the tiles. It left an arcing scarlet smear that created a perimeter with a narrow opening along the bottom. Further strokes were added. Some short. Others much longer. Some lines led to the centre. Others veered away to create dead ends.

Minotaur, as Christopher Wynn, had sketched this maze a thousand times, using paints, chalks, crayons, and charcoal. His preference, since childhood, had been a soft graphite pencil, but working with blood was so much more satisfying.

CHAPTER FIFTY

David's cab driver was a pasty-faced fellow with bad skin. The shoulders of his dark sweater were peppered with dandruff, making it look like a poor man's map of the stars. Live commentary of a Champion's League match filled the speeding vehicle. An exuberant commentator reeled off players' names as the ball was kicked around in midfield, with neither team able to break the deadlock. A lifetime ago David might have engaged the cabby in conversation about either side's chances. But with his mind filled with thoughts of torture and murder, the game could not have mattered less.

Upon arrival in Harwood, David had found the nearest mobile phone store and signed up to a new contract. He had no interest in the state-of-the-art infinity screen or impressive megapixel camera, all he needed was its GPS. Tapping the Maps icon, he watched the on-screen image orient itself and zero in on his location. They were about to enter the Shadwell Estate.

David glanced past the driver to see they were approaching three tower blocks. Looming silhouettes studded with squares of golden light. Flags and football scarves hung in windows and from balconies. Clothes pegged out on washing lines fluttered in the evening breeze. Dwarfed below the monoliths was the first of many roads filled with identical semi-detached houses.

As David tracked his approach to Claremont Road, he heard the wail of sirens. Two police cars sped past, momentarily bathing the cab's interior in flickering blue light.

A few minutes later, David settled the fare. He glanced up and down along Claremont Road. Lights were on in most of the houses. Curtains were drawn and blinds shut. The only sound was the wail of a restless infant. There were no late-night dog walkers or joggers around. David was alone on the street with only déjà vu, and a creeping sense of dread for company. He slung the bag of tools over his shoulder and ambled, as nonchalantly as he could manage, along the pavement.

Number 29 was in darkness. The glow from the nearest streetlamp illuminated a few strides past the front gate. David's heart raced as he lifted the rusty latch and stepped onto the pathway. The front door was fitted with a tarnished brass knocker in the shape of a lion's head. Unzipping the bag, David took out the hammer and slid it, grip end first, into the sleeve of his hoodie. With its steel head cradled in his palm the shaft would slip into his hand with a flick of the wrist.

He raised his other hand to knock but was suddenly consumed by doubt. If this was indeed the killer's front door, David was laughably ill-prepared for what might happen next. His plan, such as it was, had been to find Minotaur and make him talk by any means necessary. But David was nothing more than a history buff with a bag of tools that still bore their price tags. He could barely use a hammer to mend a fence, never mind smashing a man's kneecap.

"You have to... finish it."

Frank's words had been barely audible, but rang in David's head, nonetheless. They had set him off on this fool's quest, but could he bring himself to do the unthinkable? He was about to find out. Grasping the lion's head knocker, he rapped the brass plate three times and waited. Seconds ticked by, becoming a minute, but the door remained unopened. David knocked again but the house was in darkness and there were no sounds from inside. All the signs indicated there was no one home.

A shoulder-high fence separated number 29 from its immediate neighbour. As David made his way to the rear of the property, a security light next door flicked on. He froze as if a dozen high velocity rifles were trained on him. The dazzling illumination revealed David's surroundings in all their dubious glory. He was standing on a drainage cover halfway along a path of algae-coated paving slabs. Bags of rubbish were heaped against an old bed frame and a musty roll of carpet. David squeezed past the detritus into the back garden.

Once he was clear of the motion sensor the light flicked off. He dug out his new phone and thumbed on its torch. The wide-eyed face it illuminated caused David to pull back in shock, but it was his own reflection. Peering closer he saw the kitchen window. Further along was a back door. David pressed his face to the glass and saw a long-handled key on the other side.

Letting the hammer slip from his sleeve he swung its metal head into the bottom-left corner of the pane. It shattered on impact. Shards fell away, allowing David to reach in, turn the key, and enter.

The smell that permeated number 29 was like bad stew. A combination of age-old damp, decay, and something far more unpleasant. David put a hand over his nose and mouth but could still taste the fetid air. The tiny halo of light from his phone picked out a chopping board and a blender on the worktop, a child's sippy cup on the refrigerator, and dozens of egg cups lining a high shelf.

David moved from the kitchen into the hallway. Somewhere

in the house a clock was ticking. There was a resonance to the sound that suggested age and quality. Elsewhere, the house was in silence. David glanced into what he assumed was the lounge or living room. The curtains were drawn and there were no spots of light from a television or stereo system.

He climbed the stairs, aware that with every step the air grew more pungent. His grip tightened around the hammer, ready to swing at the first sign of movement. As he reached the top of the stairs the tiny beam blinked off. The phone had worked out of the box because of a partial charge. Enough to get a new user up and running but not much else.

The combination of GPS usage and powering the torch had drained its cells. David cursed himself for not purchasing a flashlight earlier that day. Pocketing the device, he fingered his way through the gloom until he located a wall switch. It flicked on, flooding the landing with sickly light from a bulb that was fluffy with cobwebs.

There were three doors along the landing, all of which were shut. The closest, he suspected, was the bathroom. The others, almost certainly, were bedrooms. Turning the second door's handle he entered a room that was illuminated by the glow of a monitor. The screensaver gave the impression of movement through a long corridor with stone walls and flickering torches.

Every so often the view flicked left or right to herald a change of direction. Straight ahead. Right turn. Straight ahead. Left turn. Straight ahead. On and on it went, becoming a hypnotic blur of digital flame and stone. This was a journey through a maze. A three-dimensional coded rendering of the bloody image David had found on his son's bedroom wall.

He approached the computer as if it might be rigged to explode. Tapping the keyboard prompted a login screen to appear. The password seemed obvious.

Minotaur.

Invalid password. You have two attempts remaining.

David tried again, this time using the word Labyrinth.

Invalid password. You have one attempt remaining.

A third erroneous password would lock the system. Could it be Ariadne's Thread, Daedalus, or something else? With everything riding on this final attempt he went with his gut instinct, Ariadnesthread.

His finger was a hair's width from pressing Enter when he stopped and deleted what he had just typed. The Minotaur killings represented a route through the maze. But while Ariadne's Thread now seemed the most logical password, it was not the most cryptic. Slowly and deliberately, David typed in the anagram, Darrianhestead and pressed Enter.

The screensaver disappeared to be replaced by the standard desktop arrangement of icons. There was a search engine and various bundled software applications. In the top-right corner was the distinctive Other Life icon, but what caught David's attention was a folder called The Maze. He slid the cursor across the screen and double-clicked. Thirteen sub-folders appeared. Each had been assigned the name of a Minotaur victim.

Juggling his need to know, with the fear of discovery, David clicked the 'Zoe Knight' archive. It contained dozens of files. Photos of him and his family gathered from social media, literary magazines, and the press. Interviews to publicise *The Rebel King* and other books he had written. There were maps of Little Dibden, photographs of the cottage, and scans of pages from a notepad. They were crammed with spiky writing and pencil sketches of him, Zoe, and Charlie.

The folder also contained a single video file represented by a thumbnail image. David recognised it as his own front door. Ignoring a wave of nausea, he double-clicked the icon. A media player showing a grainy view of the cottage appeared. There was no sound. All David could hear was the whirr of the computer's internal fan and his own breathing.

The footage was shot at head height and distorted by occasional motion blurring and diagonal flashes of rain. The porch light flared like a supernova, drowning the aperture in light before dissipating. Minotaur's gloved hand entered the frame and knocked. Ten seconds passed, then twenty.

Finally, the door opened by the few inches allowed by their security chain. A portion of Zoe's bathrobe was visible through the narrow gap. The camera tilted upwards as Minotaur lifted his head.

David's pulse quickened as he saw his wife staring directly at him, a wary look on her face. Tears prickled David's eyes as he touched the screen, as if to stroke her cheek.

"Hello," she said. "Can I help you?"

CHAPTER FIFTY-ONE

The allotments were in darkness. A cloying gloom most sensible-minded folk would have gone out of their way to avoid. Minotaur had no such quibbles. He did not need the squeak of a rusting weathervane or the gentle donk-dunk-donk of a bamboo wind chime, to know he was heading in the right direction. He unlocked the potting shed and closed the door. The dull beam of his penlight illuminated dust motes spiralling around him.

Minotaur slid the hunting knife from its scabbard and wedged its blade between two floor slats. Prising one away he reached into the void to retrieve his laptop and notebook. Both items were swaddled in bubble wrap against the dank conditions. Before leaving the flat he had retrieved the miniature cameras. They would be destroyed along with the laptop, but not before driving a sturdy nail through its hard drive.

The torch beam picked out a thermal bag bearing the logo of an online delivery service. Wynn stripped out of his bloody clothes and changed into the disguise he had stashed inside. Chinos, a pale-blue waterproof, and a motorcycle helmet bearing the same patented logo. As he filled the bag with discarded garments and equipment, he heard the distant wail of sirens. The first responders were less than a minute away.

The moped was stashed in shrubbery near the allotment's main entrance. Minotaur hauled it from the shadowy foliage, attached the thermal box to its rear fixing, and wheeled the sleek e-vehicle onto the road. Minotaur pushed the helmet over his head and flipped down the visor. With a gentle breeze caressing the lower portion of his face and the little engine buzzing quietly beneath him, he took a moment to savour his accomplishment. Despite the setbacks he had fulfilled his objective, claimed his trophies and was on his way home.

Home.

To most people the word conjured up feelings of comfort and security. A home should be a safe place, filled with happy memories and that ultimate commodity – love. Number 29 Claremont Road failed to tick any of those boxes.

CHAPTER FIFTY-TWO

1978
Everything changed after young Christopher walked in on his mother and Alan having sex. The accusation and his subsequent punishment recalibrated the household dynamic. Daphne continued to ensure he was washed, dressed and ready for school every morning. She cooked him dinner, allowed him to watch an hour of television in the evening. But once his homework was out of the way he was packed off to his bedroom.

He had become an inconvenience. Like a puppy with an incurable bowel infection. If nothing else, this new way of life, however lonely and loveless, brought an end to those Saturday afternoon trips to the shed. Sometimes Christopher would catch his stepfather watching him. Alan's eyes would linger for a moment or two before flicking away, back to whatever cop show he happened to be watching. His repugnant urges were either suppressed or he had discovered some other outlet.

In the months that followed, Alan spent an increasing amount of time away from the house. And not just in the pub, or at the bookies. He would disappear for days, sometimes weeks. Even his drinking buddies in The Crown would have no clue as to his whereabouts. On the rare occasions he made an appearance, he would be distant and moody. The slightest mishap or wrong word causing him to fly into an unholy rage. And then one day he was gone. For good this time, taking Daphne's savings and jewellery with him.

CHAPTER FIFTY-THREE

"How reliable is Jamie Hyde?" Loveday had eschewed his usual colour co-ordinated shirt and tie combination in favour of a fleece. To Rybak, this was further evidence he was losing his way.

"He's a vulnerable young man. Highly suspicious of the police and society in general. It's not surprising, given how he's been treated. But he has no reason to lie."

"Is he a user?"

"No."

"Is he...? You know, special?"

"If you mean, is he on the spectrum? Then, no."

"Are you sure about that?"

"He was lucid, focused and articulate throughout the conversation. He has a clear memory of the night in question and without him we would never have found the inhaler cap."

"*An* inhaler cap."

"I'm sorry, Guv?"

"You found *an* inhaler cap. As far as I'm aware you have yet to establish that it was taken from the Knights' home."

"We're expecting results from the fingerprint analysis any time now."

"And what does the boy's father have to say? Does he recognise it?"

"We haven't spoken to him yet."

"Why not?"

"I saw him at the hospital earlier today. I assumed he went back to the Merriweathers, but they haven't seen him."

"What about Crocker?"

"He couldn't help."

"I'll bet he couldn't." Loveday made no attempt to hide his contempt for David Knight's father-in-law. "Tell me again about the two people Hyde claims to have seen."

"Both were IC1 adult males. One was around six feet tall and average build. Jamie didn't see his face. The other was taller, maybe six three or six four, and much larger, with long hair. Again, Jamie couldn't see his face because it was obscured... by... a..." Her words faded away leaving the senior detective to stare at her expectantly. A connection that had been skulking around in Rybak's mind chose that moment to reveal itself. "Raspberry bullseye."

"I'm sorry, what?"

"Jamie Hyde said the larger man's face was hidden by an umbrella. A big red-and-white umbrella. He said it reminded him of a raspberry bullseye. It's a type of boiled sweet."

"I know what a raspberry bullseye is, thank you. Why is it important?"

"There was an umbrella just like that at Vaughan's scrapyard."

"As I recall you didn't find anything there."

"No, but Shelley Vaughan has a criminal record going way back. Drugs, shoplifting, disorderly conduct, aggravated assault. The list goes on. As for her uncle–"

Loveday closed his eyes and pinched the bridge of his nose. "For the love of all things holy, please tell me you've got more to go on than a hunch."

"Let me have another go at her."

Loveday's eyes snapped open. "No! Absolutely not. This case is hanging by a thread as it is. I don't need you 'having another go at her' and exposing us to accusations of police harassment."

"But Guv—"

"Bring me something with more meat on its bones than an umbrella and we'll talk again. Until then, stay away from Shelley Vaughan. Do you understand?"

"Yes, Guv."

Rybak left the office, angry at herself rather than Loveday. If the roles were reversed, she would have reacted the same way. What had she been thinking? Loveday was never going to sign off on something so tenuous as an umbrella.

But, she thought, *that doesn't mean I'm wrong.*

Rybak caught Prakesh's eye. "Heard anything from the lab?"

"Not yet."

"Right." She picked up the desk phone and jabbed in a number. "Here goes nothing." There was a look of grim determination on her face as she surveyed the office. Weary detectives were typing up reports with the same, dispirited hunt-and-peck technique. Prakesh mouthed the word 'tea' and mimed holding a cup which he tilted to his mouth. She gave him a thumbs up but would not be expecting much. Prakesh was a good copper, but his tea- and coffee-making skills left much to be desired.

"Come on," she murmured, biting her thumbnail. The admin staff would have clocked off long ago. The best she could hope for was some postgraduate oik who had drawn the short straw.

"Hello?" The voice was male and sounded as monotonous as the dial tone it had replaced.

"This is DI Rybak at Carlton Bridge nick. I need the results on a red-flag job I put through earlier today."

"Is this about the inhaler cap?"

"Yes," said Rybak eagerly.

"I need to put you on hold for a moment."

Before Rybak could protest, tinkly muzak kicked in. Her gaze moved to Loveday who was also on the phone. They locked eyes but there was no acknowledgement on either side. Instead, the senior investigator slid his chair sideways and pulled the blinds closed.

"Hello?" The man with the dull voice had returned. "I have the results right here. Would you like me to–?"

"Yes!"

As he ran through the usual boilerplate guff about spectral analysis, she heard the buzz of a nearby phone. Then another from across the office. Her own phone chimed, joining the chorus of ringtones. "Sorry to cut you short but I need the bottom line. Were any fingerprints identified, other than those belonging to the Knight family?"

Prakesh dashed back into the office, apparently having left the teas unmade. His eyes were wide and glued to his phone's screen.

"Please," said Rybak, attuned to the sudden shift in the atmosphere around her. "I need a yes or no. Did you find any–?"

"No."

"Shit!" With no time for chit-chat, she hung up. "Vik? What's going on?"

Prakesh spun his phone round so she could see what he, and everyone else, was reading: **Home Invasion Leaves Two Dead**.

"Is it him?"

"It just says both victims died from wounds sustained at the scene."

"Both?"

"That's what it says."

"Can I have everyone's attention?" Loveday's booming voice made everyone look around. "No doubt you've seen the latest headlines. Well, I've just heard these Harwood murders have been officially classified as Minotaur killings."

Rybak shook her head, struggling with this latest turn of events. "Two victims in one night? That doesn't sound like our guy."

Loveday continued. "One of the victims was a white, middle-aged female. Both breasts were removed. The second victim was an IC3 male. A neighbour who probably heard a disturbance and went to help."

"What about the maze? Did they find one?"

Loveday nodded and swept an exasperated hand along his face. "I'll know more by morning prayers tomorrow. Look, whatever the press throws at us, I know everyone in this room is giving their all. Stay focused. We will get him."

Rybak approached Loveday as a discussion erupted around them.

"Guv? I just spoke to the lab."

"And?"

"Nothing."

"It was always going to be a long shot."

"I'll uh..." began Rybak, trying to think of something vaguely constructive to say. "I'll crack on then."

"Wait. This hunch of yours. Give me one good reason why I should let you run with it?"

"Guv, with all due respect, you don't have many other options."

CHAPTER FIFTY-FOUR

As expected, no one gave him a second look. The sight of a motorbike courier delivering food orders was as much a part of modern life as broadband, selfies and Botox. Minotaur's route took him several miles north of the Shadwell Estate, extending his return journey to Claremont Street by more than an hour. On the flipside, anyone attempting to track him would be led a merry dance. His route would take him through an area of Harwood with several convenient CCTV blind spots.

The news would have broken by now. Across the world, mobile phones would be pinging with bulletins about another Minotaur murder. Reporters and camera crews from the major networks would be flocking to the Shadwell Estate. Two murders in one night meant sweet Kim and that steroid-enhanced lump would be considered his Elizabeth Stride and Catherine Eddowes – Jack the Ripper's infamous Double Event. That alone would be enough to whip the media into a frenzy.

With lurid headlines swirling in his mind, Minotaur took a left turn into Bleechers Lane. Beyond the fluorescent light of an all-night grocery store, the narrow road was cloaked in darkness.

Up ahead was The Smuggler's Dog, a once popular spit and sawdust drinking den. A far cry from the trendy gin bars a quarter of a mile away. Now it was a smoke-blackened husk. Fire had ripped through this back pocket of Harwood five years earlier. With no political will to do anything but turn a blind eye, the area had been left to rot.

Minotaur switched off the moped's single headlight and trusted his own memory of the area to guide him. The thunderous gush of water could be heard even before he rolled to a stop. Removing the helmet, he wheeled the bike along a brick alley leading to a footpath along the river. Silhouetted by moonlight was the lifting bridge that towered above Harwood Creek viaduct. In the distance, bars and nightclubs cast a blur of multicoloured lights across the horizon.

Minotaur tossed his hunting knife and the computer's hard drive into the river. There were a couple of gentle plops from somewhere in the darkness as incriminating evidence hit the water's surface and sank into its murky depths.

He flicked on the little penlight. The beam picked out a chain-link fence smothered by an aggressive mass of bindweed. Night flies buzzed around the white trumpet flowers and arrowhead leaves that hung over a stained mattress.

Minotaur dragged it aside to reveal a holdall, a mountain bike and a jerry can – items he had hidden the day before. After changing clothes and retrieving his precious trophies he doused the moped and thermal box with petrol. He struck a match and watched the flame dance a rhumba before dropping it onto the pyre. There was a satisfying whoosh as the accelerant ignited.

CHAPTER FIFTY-FIVE

From start to finish the video lasted just eight minutes but watching it felt like a lifetime. If Zoe had died from that first hammer blow, David might have taken some comfort in knowing it had at least been quick. But it had taken a second blow to kill her. Zoe's left eye stared, moist, and unblinking, at the camera. A red blob stained the eggshell white of her sclera.

A gloved hand grabbed Zoe's hair and proceeded to drag the body upstairs. Her swollen belly bucked with every upward step. David could not help but wonder if, by this point, his unborn child had still been alive. Tears blurred his vision as Zoe was bundled into the bathtub. The killer's hands reappeared. One held a gleaming knife. The other pulled aside the folds of Zoe's bathrobe to reveal her silky nightdress.

Watching the brutality that followed was David's penance for not being there to protect his family. As the blade performed its cruel work, he felt the last shreds of his humanity disintegrate. It was the strangest sensation. As if it were carried away by a gentle breeze. Any doubt that he might not be able to do what was necessary had vanished.

When the butchering was done, David returned to the

landing. By the skirting was an extension cable which trailed across the carpet from a wall socket. Its flex ended with a dusty hub into which four air fresheners were plugged. They were positioned outside the third door, but their lavender fragrance fell way short of masking the abominable stench.

A long shackle padlock hung from a metal hasp screwed into the door. David looked at it for several seconds, realising what it could mean. Pushing an ear to one of the panels he listened for sounds from inside. "Charlie? It's Daddy."

He dropped the bag and slammed his hands against the grubby woodwork. "Charlie? Say something. Talk to me."

David gave the padlock a sharp tug, but it refused to budge. He raised the hammer and brought it down hard. The hasp buckled but held firm. He struck again but missed and dented the doorframe. His third attempt wrenched out the topmost screws leaving the latch resting at an angle. Slotting the hammer's twin claws into position David levered downwards. The last two screws popped out with minimal effort. The padlock fell away, landing between his feet.

Upon entering the room, David was hit by a sensory overload. The pungent smell was compounded by a flashing light and the constant buzz of white noise. A cathode ray television was the source. Its aerial jack had been pulled out, filling the screen with static. A patchwork of noise-dampening material covered the floor, walls, ceiling, and window. Layers of polystyrene, cardboard, vinyl sheeting and a mass of foam rubber.

The flickering glow illuminated a vaguely humanoid shape in the middle of the room. Against all logic and reason, the figure appeared to be floating.

CHAPTER FIFTY-SIX

The man was suspended by a cat's cradle of chains bolted at symmetrical points to the wall and ceiling joists. They ended in leather straps, padded with foam loops to reduce the chafing around his wrists and ankles. His chest, torso and upper thighs were supported by a canvas hammock, ensuring the incumbent's weight was evenly distributed.

He looked to be in his late seventies. A mop of lank grey hair framed a horse-like face. His lips were cracked and the colour of uncooked chicken. At the sight of David, he unleashed a bestial grunt and his face contorted in a series of tics and spasms. The man became increasingly fractious, rocking backwards and forwards amongst the clinking chains.

"I want to help you," David said, "but you have to calm down."

The man gave no indication that he understood. His bony limbs flinched and jolted as if he were in the grip of a seizure. It looked as if the killer had kept this poor soul locked up for years. It was small wonder his mind had turned to mush. Apart from the buzzing TV the only other object in the room was a wardrobe.

David opened its cherry wood doors and recoiled at the thing inside. A withered, ash-grey husk with wiry hair and a pair of gaping eye sockets. It had been bent double, shoved into the enclosed space, and left to decompose. Rigor mortis followed by bloating, decay and finally, skeletonisation. Material that had once been a nightdress had fused to the remains. In the months following death, a noxious mix of enzymes had leaked from every orifice. The juices stained the fabric, rendering its delicate flowery design almost imperceptible.

CHAPTER FIFTY-SEVEN

1**983**
    Christopher Wynn left school with no qualifications. He took whatever work came his way, however menial, to make ends meet. By this time, Daphne was bedbound. Morose and reliant on her son to feed and wash her. Christopher rarely slept. Most nights were spent teaching himself to code with a 48k ZX Spectrum.

The printed letters and numbers on those little rubber keys eventually wore away but the effort paid off. His first electronic version of the maze evolved into a game he called Minotaur. It was a text adventure that brought the labyrinth to life by describing its stone corridors, flickering torches, and numerous traps in vivid detail. It prompted the intrepid user to go left, right, backward, or straight on. The aim of the game was to navigate a route to the centre while avoiding the ever-present threat of a monstrous bull-man.

Aged just seventeen, Wynn secured a meeting with one of the biggest movers and shakers in the UK's gaming industry. John Fenton-Davis, or JFD as he was widely known. A millionaire by the age of twenty-three, JFD was the genius responsible for some of the most successful run-and-jump platform games. He was looking to expand his label just as the Minotaur game pinged on his radar.

JFD bought the rights for a tidy sum and gave Wynn a small but crucial percentage of all future profits. The game was released to huge acclaim and became an instant hit with the sword and sorcery brigade. The splashy cover art of its cassette case featured the titular beast brandishing a sword in a mighty, two-handed grip.

JFD had big plans to fast-track a follow-up before other gaming houses came knocking at Wynn's door. He wanted a second maze. "Make it more elaborate!" he demanded. "I want more traps and more Minotaurs."

Alas, lightning did not strike twice. Lacking the necessary inspiration, Wynn's deadline came and went. The job of coding a sequel went to someone much less talented. For the briefest time, Christopher Wynn's star had shone so very brightly. He would never again experience that same level of success, or code another best-selling game.

The royalty cheques dwindled as computing power and demand for more sophisticated gaming experiences increased. Minotaur became a curio, existing in the substrata of fondly remembered, but not quite classic games.

CHAPTER FIFTY-EIGHT

Squeezing the brakes, Minotaur screeched to a halt outside number 29 Claremont Road. He swung the front gate open and wheeled his bike to the porch. Batting away a dangling wisteria tendril he opened the front door and manhandled the bike inside. He switched on the hallway light and scooped up an envelope that had been stuffed through the letterbox. Another final demand to add to his collection. Shrugging off his rucksack he went straight to the kitchen. It was long past Alan's feeding time, and the old man would be wailing for his sippy cup.

Minotaur took out the freezer bag containing Kim's breasts. He was about to slide the contents onto the chopping board when he noticed movement by the back door. A flap of stripey curtain wafted inwards. He pulled the curtain aside to reveal the broken pane of glass. Suddenly on high alert, the killer turned around to find himself staring into the eyes of a maniac.

David was already in mid-swing. The hammer crunched into the side of Minotaur's head. He remained upright for a moment before staggering sideways and slamming into the worktop. One hand lashed out, knocking over the plastic jug.

Pink mush splashed across the linoleum in a wide arc. Minotaur sunk to his knees, spit bubbling from his lips, while staring defiantly at David – his very own Theseus.

CHAPTER FIFTY-NINE

1995

Wynn smothered Daphne with one of her own pillows. The old woman struggled at first but then lay still, apparently accepting her fate. When it was done, Wynn arranged his mother's arms around him in an approximation of a hug. Being so close felt good. The safest place in the world.

"I love you, Mum." He brushed aside a wayward strand of hair to kiss her forehead.

He slept well that night but when he woke up, her body was cold and beginning to stiffen. Shuffling away from the chilly embrace he retrieved the family album from the top of her wardrobe. The hefty book had a leather effect cover, its pages separated by slivers of translucent paper. Faded pictures of family trips, holidays, birthdays, and Christmases. Wynn barely recognised himself as a happy-go-lucky youngster.

Then there was a noticeable time jump. The period between his father leaving, and Alan appearing on the scene. There was a single, secondary school photograph of Christopher looking pale and sullen. Other pictures were of his stepfather.

Alan was either pictured alone – usually in a pub, clutching a pint of beer – or slobbering over Daphne.

2009

It cost Wynn a considerable chunk of his savings to find Alan. His stepfather was good at avoiding his debtors, many of whom were prone to violence. He had moved from town to town and changed his name several times. Running up bar bills and borrowing from gullible women. Wynn travelled the country, visiting pub after pub, and showing a picture of his stepfather to those he met along the way. His search eventually led him to Southend-on-Sea. A stone's throw from the world's longest pleasure pier. Down a side street that was notorious for its obliging prostitutes.

When his stepfather finally emerged from his low-rent bedsit, it was obvious the years had not been kind to him.

"Hello Alan. Long time, no see."

Alan's journey back to consciousness had been like reaching for a speck of light a thousand miles away. He was vaguely aware of shapes in the darkness. Strange and ethereal. Their edges a blur. Indistinct tendrils of colour bleeding through, like ink molecules swirling in water. He tried to move but his body refused to play ball. Was he simply too weak or had his brain been scrambled like an egg in a pan?

When the colours settled, and his environment slipped into focus, he could see he was in a room, lit by a single light bulb. Empty except for a wardrobe he recognised. The floor, the walls and the ceiling were covered in flattened cardboard and sheets of foam rubber. All secured in place with silvery lengths of criss-crossing duct tape. His eyeline was higher than normal and he was angled towards the floor. There was pressure on his thighs, midriff, and upper arms as if he were dangling like a puppet. And what was that infernal stench?

"Help!"

He waited a few moments before calling again. "Is anyone there?"

A door, hidden amongst the material affixed to the wall, swung open. His stepson – now a man – entered the room.

"Chrissy! What the fuck are you playing at?" Alan struggled against his bonds, setting the chains clinking and clanking. "Get me down!"

"I'm sorry, Alan, but that's not going to happen. These four walls are your world now. You will never breathe fresh air again or see another living soul other than me. I will feed you; I will clean you, and I will keep you alive. But whatever time you have left will be miserable and filled with suffering. Scream all you want. Please – go right ahead. No one will hear you. No one's coming to help. It's just you and me now." He paused long enough to open the wardrobe door. "Oh, and Mum."

Alan stared at the shrivelled ash-grey horror that had once been his wife.

"And if you ever call me 'Chrissy' again, I will cut your lips off and feed them to you."

In the early days of his captivity, Alan rebelled by the only means available to him – a hunger strike. He clamped his lips shut and turned his head away or spat the frothy liquid out in disgust. But as his body consumed itself to sustain his most vital organs, Alan relented. He was too much of a coward to die of self-imposed starvation.

Weeks turned to months and months turned to years. During that time, Wynn's obsession with the maze intensified. Drawings, paintings, and online variants were not enough. He needed more.

CHAPTER SIXTY

The flattened cardboard was covered in age-old puke and bloodstains. It was the first thing Minotaur saw upon regaining consciousness. He understood his predicament immediately. The way he was suspended above the floor and how the slightest movement set chains rattling. It could mean only one thing. He craned his neck sideways. Sure enough, he could see Alan's spindly legs in his peripheral vision.

David had found Minotaur's keys and used them to release Alan. The old man's limbs had atrophied so badly they were like a pair of wet noodles. His malnourished body was jaundiced and mottled with sores. He was naked but for a bulging diaper that showed signs of leakage around its elasticated legs. David placed the old man in a sitting position against the wall. His head lolled from side to side, threatening to snap the vertebrae in his thin neck.

"I know you." Minotaur's words were a rage-filled hiss. In the middle of his forehead was a violent purple welt and his right eye had developed a noticeable twitch. The rest of his face was covered in dried blood from the injury he had rushed to patch up.

"And I know you, motherfucker." David thumbed the box-cutter's blade into position. "I should thank you. This is the perfect set-up for what I have in mind."

"And what do you have in mind, David?"

"I'm going to ask you a question. If I think you're lying, or you refuse to answer, I will cut you."

"In that case you'd better ask it then, hadn't you?"

"Where's my son?"

"Ah, of course. That question. The thing is, you may think you have it all figured out – standing there with your blade and your hammer and whatever other little toys you have stashed away – but you really do not have a clue."

"No? Why's that?"

"Because you're not the one in control."

David ripped the plaster off Minotaur's cheek to reveal a deep wound and a glistening clot. "Looks nasty. Let's even things up, shall we?"

The blade sank into the killer's other cheek. David dragged it downwards towards his captive's lower jaw. Six centimetres of flesh split apart and ran with blood. Minotaur bucked and jolted but succeeded only in pivoting wildly.

David wiped the knife on his prisoner's shoulder. "Much better. Now answer the question."

Minotaur glared at David. "You'll have to remind me. What is it you want to know?"

David unleashed his best right hook. The blow landed, shattering a bone in the killer's nose. "Where's my son?"

Minotaur snorted, coughed, and spat. A ragged splash of crimson saliva hit the padding by David's feet. "He's a cute kid. You must love him very much."

Swapping the box-cutter for pliers, David removed the killer's shoes and socks. Minotaur tried to peer over his shoulder, but movement was restricted by the harness. David's intention soon became clear. Cold steel jaws clamped around the base of Minotaur's smallest toe.

"Where is my son?"

"It was your fault, David. You know that don't–?"

His words became a scream as the metal snipped shut and his toe fell to the floor.

"Where is my son?"

"You..." rasped Minotaur. "You..." He paused as the pliers closed around the next toe along.

"Where is my son?"

"If you had only been there when I–"

Another snip. Another scream.

"Where is my son?"

CHAPTER SIXTY-ONE

The scrapyard gates were padlocked. Rybak gave the chain an exploratory rattle to no avail. Her view of the demountable office was limited but, as far as she could tell, there was no one around. She returned to the Audi, shielding her eyes as a flash of early morning sunlight reflected off the windscreen. Prakesh was behind the wheel, hanging up on a call.

Rybak slipped into the passenger seat. "Any word yet on Knight?"

"Mrs Merriweather said he hasn't been back or even called."

Rybak dug a long-forgotten packet of mints from her duffle coat. She peeled away the wrapping with the focus of someone defusing a ticking bomb. "Jenrick told him something. I'm sure of it. Now he's running around playing detective. Call it in. We need him picked up, sharpish." She popped a sweet in her mouth and sucked on it ruminatively. "Let's try Vaughan's home address."

Prakesh shifted into gear and pulled away from the scrapyard. "So, how do we play this? We haven't exactly got anything on her, have we?"

"No, but she doesn't know that. Let's shake the tree and see what falls out."

Shelley Vaughan lived with her uncle in what might charitably be referred to as a smallholding. A more accurate description would be five acres of mud and chicken shit. The Audi's suspension was pushed to breaking point as it bumped and crunched along an unmade road. Trailing branches and brambles scraped along the vehicle's roof and bodywork as it approached a ramshackle bungalow.

The detectives' arrival was heralded by the frenzied yapping of dogs. As Rybak and Prakesh exited the vehicle, two bug-eyed pugs came hurtling out of the foliage. Bringing up the rear was a lumbering Staffordshire bull terrier with a demonic face and drool-covered teeth.

"Oh shit!" yelled Prakesh as the two smaller dogs leapt up at him with scant regard for physics. There was a panicked look on his face as the gnashing canines pogoed in front of him.

"Vik? Stay calm." Despite her best efforts, Rybak sounded less than convincing. She was having her own showdown with the bull terrier. It closed in on her. Ears flat to its head. A low growl rattling the back of its throat.

"Caesar!" Shelley Vaughan's shrill voice called out. "Pumpkin! Barnaby! Get here! Now!" Contempt for her unexpected visitors further distorted Shelley's naturally rat-like features. She wore a faded Wham! T-shirt, and a pair of leopard print leggings that did nothing to conceal her bandy lower limbs. "What do you want?"

"We have a few follow-up questions," Rybak said in a voice she hoped sounded casual. "Would it be all right if we came in for a few minutes to talk?"

"Have you got another one of them search warrant things?"

Rybak cast an anxious glance at the growling hound. "No. Not this time."

"So I can tell you to sling your hook?"

"Yes, Miss Vaughan. That's correct."

Shelley snorted and spent a moment sucking on whatever it was she had dredged up. "All right. I ain't got nothing to hide." Turning away, she headed back to the bungalow. The dogs trotted along by her feet, obediently.

Rybak and Prakesh were shown into the living room. The curtains were drawn, and the smell of nicotine and dog hung heavy in the air. Along the far wall was a black ash unit housing a bulky stacking hi-fi unit. On one side was a cabinet. On the other, a set of shelves crammed with LPs.

The detectives perched on the edge of a threadbare sofa while Shelley slumped into an armchair. The pugs jumped onto her lap and curled up together. The Staffordshire bull terrier – who Shelley had called 'Caesar' – sat by her side, on high alert.

Rybak felt the intensity of the dog's beady-eyed glare.

"Nice collection."

Shelley tore open a pack of Rothmans King Size and lit one with a cheap lighter. "What?"

"I was just admiring your records. Must be worth a lot."

"Dunno. It's my Uncle Pete's. He likes all that old crap." She eyed the detectives warily before blowing twin plumes of bluish smoke from her nostrils. "So, what's this about?"

"Like I said, we have some follow-up questions."

"But you never found nothing at my place so what's there to ask?"

Prakesh glanced nervously at the dogs. "Your place? I thought your uncle owned it?"

Shelley shot the young detective an evil glare. "Christ, what is it with you lot?"

"My lot?"

"Don't twist my words. I meant you lot as in 'the filth'."

"I take it your uncle is still away?"

"Yeah. So?"

"When is he coming back?"

"I don't know! He just told me to keep an eye on things while he's gone."

"But not today."

"It's my day off. I'm allowed a day off, aren't I?"

Rybak smiled pleasantly. "Of course. Oh, and I wanted to let you know we found that car we were looking for. The Subaru."

"Case closed then, eh?"

"Not quite. Finding the vehicle opened a new line of inquiry. One that led us to make an interesting discovery."

Shelley had barely blown out one lungful of smoke before sucking down another. Her bony knee jiggled up and down. Rybak recognised it as classic anxiety displacement. The movement was enough to disturb the flat-faced dogs on her lap. They looked up at her, cocking their misshapen heads plaintively.

Rybak reached into the pocket of her duffle coat and pulled out an evidence bag. She let it dangle between her thumb and forefinger.

"Am I meant to know what that is?"

"This is the cap of an asthma inhaler." Rybak gave the bag a shake for emphasis. "It belongs to a missing child."

"What's it got to do with me?"

Rybak returned the evidence bag to her pocket. "I had it sent for analysis. You know, to check for fingerprints and whatnot. Now, I just need to get one or two things clear in my mind."

Shelley's leg froze, mid-tremble. "What sort of things?"

Rybak studied her face, soaking up every tic and micro expression. "For a start could you talk us through your movements on Tuesday the twenty-second of June."

"I've told you already."

"Yes, but if you could take us through it one more time. You might find you remember something new."

"Like I said, I was at the yard."

"All day?"

"Most of it."

"Did you have many customers?"

"No more than usual."

"But there was nothing logged in your accounts."

Ash broke away from Shelley's cigarette and fell to the carpet. "We had a few people through the gates, but they didn't end up parting with any cash. It happens."

"And what time did you finish?" said Prakesh.

"What was that again?" said Shelley. "Didn't quite catch what you said there."

"What time did you go to the lock-up?"

"What the fuck are you talking about? What lock-up? I didn't go to no fucking lock-up."

Rybak made a conciliatory gesture. "Miss Vaughan–?"

"Nah, bollocks to it." Shelley stabbed a nicotine-stained finger at the detectives. "I see what you're doing. You're trying to fit me up, but I ain't having it."

"I can assure you, that isn't our intention."

With a sweep of her hand, Shelley brushed the dogs away as she stood. "Go on, the pair of you. Get out. Fuck off!"

"We didn't mean to cause any offence. If I could just ask you to–"

"No!" Shelley bustled past them into the hallway and wrenched open the front door. "I'm not telling you again. I want you out!"

"Miss Vaughan, if we don't do it here, we'll have to–"

"Do it at the nick? That's fine by me, sweetheart. I ain't saying one more word without my brief. Now get out of my house or I'll set the dogs on you."

CHAPTER SIXTY-TWO

When David ran out of toes to amputate, he moved on to Minotaur's teeth. He started at the back, locating a prime candidate in the form of a chunky molar but it held firm despite his best efforts. He gave several others a firm tug but was unable to get the right angle or sufficient purchase and settled on a prominent canine. Spittle frothed from the killer's mouth as steel jaws clamped into position.

Sweat beaded across David's forehead, his arm cramping from the strain of pulling. Eventually he felt the tooth give a little. He eased off to watch blood oozing from Minotaur's gums. "Where is my son?"

The killer's pale eyes flashed but he remained silent. The pliers resumed their grip. David clenched the tool with both hands and gave it a sharp wrench. As the canine tore free of bone and gum it made a sound like Velcro strips tearing apart. Minotaur howled as he swung away, eyes drowning in tears.

David held the tooth up for his unwilling patient to see. "Where is my son?"

Minotaur's mouth hung open, exposing his ravaged gum in

all its swollen glory. But then his body went limp as if a powerful sedative had been administered.

Minotaur retreated to his safe place. His childhood sanctuary. The maze. It had been many years since he had visited it in this way. He moved swiftly through its tunnels, flaming torch in hand, marvelling at its intricate design. So much time had gone into creating the digital equivalent he had forgotten how immersive his mind's-eye version could be.

With every change of direction, it seemed he was journeying deeper into the bowels of the earth. His skin prickled with goosebumps and his breath fogged the air.

"Where is my son?" David Knight's voice was a vague echo from far, far away.

Let him have his fun. If I'm to die, then so be it.

David staggered into the back garden and fell to his knees. He felt contaminated. Polluted by a toxicity that wire wool and bleach could not have scrubbed away.

What now? How much more pain must I inflict? Deep down he knew the answer. It could only end one way. Minotaur would die, taking Charlie's fate with him to Hell.

"There is another way."

Zoe's voice felt like velvety fingers caressing the sides of David's head. He dared not turn for fear of shattering the illusion. "Tell me! What do I have to do?"

Silence.

David hauled himself up and went back inside.

"There is another way."

What had Zoe meant by that? Was David meant to offer the killer a bribe? Try to reason with him? Or hope for some late spark of redemption?

Surveying the kitchen he saw a stack of mail on the kitchen table. It was all addressed to the same person – Daphne Wynn. Most bore the words *Final Demand* in big red letters. David opened the cupboard doors and saw shelves crammed with tinned goods, bottled water, pasta, cereal, and long-life milk.

Then he saw the freezer bag. The severed breasts lay limp and red against the polythene, next to the chopping board and food blender. His mind flashed on Zoe's ruined chest. The oval wounds. The glistening meat.

"There is another way."

Zoe's words continued to ring in his head, taunting him.

His gaze fell upon the sippy cup on the refrigerator, its plastic faded and dented. The child's vessel looked incongruous in this ghoulish environment.

Minotaur had been blending his trophies, then feeding the obscene mix to his captive. It seemed the old man was being punished for an act so heinous, death was considered too good for him.

Hairs on the back of David's neck stood rigid as a thought took shape.

Zoe had been right. There was another way.

CHAPTER SIXTY-THREE

Minotaur's pace slowed. He was no longer certain of his location. Was it possible he had taken a wrong turn? It seemed unlikely but there could be no other explanation. He retraced his steps, scanning the sandstone walls for a familiar nick or etching.

"Wynn?"

Minotaur had paid little heed to his nemesis since venturing into the maze. David Knight would have been hard at work. No doubt becoming increasingly frustrated by his lack of progress.

"Wynn! That is your name, isn't it? Time to wake up."

Minotaur ignored the distant voice. He veered left into a corridor he only vaguely recognised.

"It's the old man's feeding time. He's hungry."

Minotaur stopped, peering around as if expecting to see David standing behind him.

"I thought I'd give him something a bit different for a change, so I've added my own special ingredient. Have you heard of Ventraxotine?"

Alan's gummy mouth opened and closed upon spying the sippy cup. His tongue made expectant clicking noises like an infant craving its mother's tit.

David glanced from the frail imbecile to the deranged killer. "You took everything from me. That won't mean much to you, but I was a wreck. So, I went to my doctor and begged her to give me something to numb the pain. Nothing worked until I tried Ventraxotine. They warn you not to exceed the recommended dose because they're so strong. The thing is, I don't need them anymore. I'm not better – that's not on the cards – but I've found a new way of coping. Anyway, I don't want them going to waste, so I put them in the mix, along with a load of painkillers and other stuff I found. It should be enough to put the old boy out of his misery."

This was partly true. David had dropped the last of his pills into the blender, but Minotaur's latest trophies remained untouched. In reaching this stage, David had trampled over many of his own moral and ethical boundaries but that was one line he would never cross. Instead, he had mixed the pills with cold soup.

He raised the sippy cup, so it was almost level with the old man's flaking lips.

"No!" The killer's voice was distorted by swelling and a sudden anguish.

"Where is my son?"

David logged in to Minotaur's Other Life account using the details he had just been given. A powerful graphics card made quick work of rendering Claremont Street. David navigated the bull-headed avatar to the last place he had visited prior to his ejection – the allotment.

He found the shed and clicked to open the padlock. A single option appeared, 'Enter Code'. Selecting it brought up a second window bearing four white squares. David typed the digits – 1 9 7 8 – and pressed Enter. The padlock disappeared and the rickety door swung open to reveal a murky interior.

David guided the hulking brute inside. This was it. Minotaur's creation. His labyrinth. Anyone else would have wandered aimlessly along its corridors, but not David. He unfolded his sketch and followed the route to the central chamber.

There was no fanfare upon arrival. It was black and empty except for a media player, giving the impression of being in a darkened cinema. There were no buttons to pause, rewind or fast forward, just a panel into which live video was streamed. An image, marred by blocky pixelation, eventually snapped into focus to reveal a high-angled view of a room. Sitting cross-legged on a mattress was a small boy huddled in a dirty sheet.

Prakesh was downbeat as he and Rybak walked back to the Audi. "I'm sorry, Guv. I messed up."

Rybak glanced over her shoulder to see Shelley Vaughan glaring at them through a gap in the curtains. "It was worth a shot. We'll get a warrant and come back first thing tomorrow."

"If there's anything to be found, it'll be long gone by then."

As they reached the car the silence between them was broken by a melodic chime. Rybak pulled out her phone, assuming it would be Loveday calling to check on their progress. To her surprise, it was an unknown number. "Hello?"

"Rybak?"

"Yes? Who is this?"

"David Knight."

"David. Where are you? Are you all right?"

"I've found him."

"What?"

"I've found Charlie. I'm sending you a picture of him now."

A new message pinged in her inbox. Rybak opened it and stared at the image. "How did you get this?"

"It doesn't matter. The important thing is, that's Charlie. Look at the time and date. That's a live feed."

"Where is he?"

"I don't know, but does the name 'Vaughan' mean anything to you?"

CHAPTER SIXTY-FOUR

S helley Vaughan watched the detectives deliberating their next move. "What the fuck are they doing out there?" Her anxiety levels were dangerously close to hitting the red zone. Caesar growled as the smaller dogs played tug of war with a tatty sock. Shelley lit another cigarette and puffed on it anxiously.

The police officers were now walking back towards the bungalow. "Shit!" Shelley grabbed her phone and placed a hurried call. It was answered as Rybak knocked on the front door.

"Uncle Pete, it's me. Shelley."

"What do you want?"

"It's the filth."

"What about them?"

"They're outside."

"At the yard?"

"No! They're at your place. What do I do?"

"You keep your trap shut. That's what you do."

"I don't like it. You said it would be all right."

Shelley waited expectantly but heard only breathing. "Uncle Pete?"

A click was followed by the monotonous hum of a dial tone. With a furious screech, Shelley hurled the handset across the room. It hit the wall with a sharp crack and fell to the floor. The little dogs froze, staring bug-eyed at their owner, the saliva-drenched sock quivering between them.

"Miss Vaughan?" called the female detective. "Open the door."

Rybak peered through the letterbox. A rectangular view of the hallway was suddenly consumed by vicious snapping teeth and looping trails of dog saliva. She only just managed to pull her fingers to safety. On the other side of the door Caesar was barking and clawing splinters from the woodwork.

Rybak's plan had been to keep Shelley talking until backup arrived but with a child's life at immediate risk, her only option was to improvise. "Vik? With me, now."

She led the way through dense shrubbery along the side of the building. Progress was impeded by shoe-sucking mud and tangles of foliage. As they approached the back door Rybak shrugged off her duffle coat and wrapped it around her arm. "On three."

Prakesh nodded, pulling a cannister of pepper spray from his pocket and readying it for use. He watched the senior detective mouth a silent countdown.

One... Two... Three!

Rybak was barely inside when Caesar sprang at her, snarling and snapping. She braced herself, using the swaddled arm like a shield. Fangs sank deep into the thick fabric. The dog's impetus knocked Rybak to the floor. The huge beast landed on her, shaking its head savagely. The coarse woollen material offered Rybak some protection, but it still felt like her arm was being simultaneously crushed and torn from its socket.

Prakesh unloaded a burst of pepper spray into the dog's face. There was a sizzle as the chemical compound burnt the mucous membranes in the animal's eyes, nose, throat, and lungs. The ensuing yelp was the trigger for Prakesh to grab the dog's collar in a two-handed grip and drag it away from Rybak. Disoriented and snuffling for breath, the animal's legs freewheeled as Prakesh hauled it into the nearest room – the bathroom – and shut the door. Its bark had lost none of its viciousness but was interspersed with mewls of pain.

Watching from the living-room doorway were the two pugs. They cowered and whimpered as their alpha was stripped of its authority.

Prakesh helped Rybak to her feet. "Are you all right, Guv?"

"I'm fine, but watch your back."

David, still clutching his barely charged phone, stared at the monitor. Charlie had curled into the foetal position and was sucking his thumb. The boy had lost weight and his hair, which resembled a bird's nest at the best of times, was even shaggier than usual.

Rybak had confirmed that someone named Vaughan was a person of interest but had been reticent to say much else. David, for his part, had sidestepped her questions, promising to hand himself in only when Charlie was safe. It was a deal Rybak had no choice but to accept.

On the screen, Charlie sat up. He looked agitated as a second person entered the room. The child backed away, clearly terrified. A dark shape moved in front of the lens, obscuring

David's view. He jabbed the volume up to its highest position but all he could hear was a hiss of static.

A woman with a mean face and curly hair grabbed the boy and twisted him into a chokehold. She whispered something which sent the child into a panic. His little legs kicked out, but he was no match for his captor.

CHAPTER SIXTY-FIVE

"Charlie Knight? Can you hear me?"

Rybak checked the second of two bedrooms. The walls were adorned with posters of Madonna, Prince, and Michael Jackson. Dirty clothes and pizza boxes littered the floor. There were only three possible hiding places. Behind the door, under the bed and in the wardrobe. Rybak searched them all but found no trace of their suspect.

She returned to the hallway where Prakesh was clambering down from a loft ladder. He flicked off his LED tactical-style torch and shook his head. Rybak checked her watch. The support units were only a few minutes away but even that was too long.

Striding back into the living room she scanned the floor, the ceiling, and the walls. "Charlie? This is the police. If you can hear me, shout. Let me know where you are." All she could hear was furious howling from Caesar.

One of the smaller dogs trotted over to the black ash unit and whimpered as it pawed the cabinet.

Prakesh's eyes flicked down to the animal. "Guv?"

Rybak followed his line of sight before looking back at him, the penny dropping. "Shoo!" she said, clapping her hands. "Go on, scram!" The pug did not fancy its chances against this new alpha so scurried away to join the other little dog.

Prakesh pulled the black ash door open. There was nothing inside, just a back panel. At first glance it seemed perfectly normal — until he switched on his torch. The beam illuminated a cluster of greasy handprints along one side of the dark hardboard and two hinges along the other. He gave it a push and the panel swung inwards. The unit was positioned against a fake wall. Floor-to-ceiling timber joists covered by plasterboard.

Rybak followed Prakesh into a cramped passageway that ran the width of the living room. The torchlight panned along bare floorboards before settling on a door. A deadbolt had been slotted into its open position. Fingers closing around the handle Prakesh pushed down, and the door swung open.

Shelley Vaughan was in the secret room, her arm tight around Charlie Knight's neck. "You stay away from me! I'll kill him! I will! I'll fucking kill him."

Prakesh slid into the room, holding his hands up to show he was unarmed.

Rybak remained in the doorway, eyes fixed on the boy. She flashed him an encouraging smile. "You must be Charlie. It's going to be all right. I promise."

"Shut your mouth! You ain't calling the shots here."

Rybak continued as if Shelley was not even there. "I'm a detective. You know what a detective is, don't you, Charlie? It means I'm here to help you."

"I'm warning you! Shut your mouth, pig!"

Rybak gave the woman a steely glare. "Do you want to know what I think, Shelley? I think you know this is over and that you're in a lot of trouble. You don't want to hurt the boy, do you? That will just make a bad situation a whole lot worse."

Shelley Vaughan's pinched expression flickered, as if

realising she was cornered, while her uncle was off sunning himself.

"Come on, Shelley. We can work together on this, but what you do next will determine how this goes for you."

"I... I didn't want any of it. It was my Uncle Pete. It was all him."

"We can talk about that later but first I need you to let go of Charlie."

Shelley's wiry body went limp, and her arms fell away from the boy.

Rybak knelt so she was on Charlie's level and opened her arms in a welcoming gesture.

CHAPTER SIXTY-SIX

Tears rolled down David's cheeks as he watched his son run to the detective. Rybak's arms closed around the boy, an expression of unbridled relief on her face. She pointed up at the camera and mouthed something like, *Look up there*. Charlie obliged, giving David the best view yet of his son.

The child was a ghost of his former self. All trace of the mischievous little scamp David knew and loved was gone. In his place was a cowed waif. Shadows stained a thin face that was locked in an expression of mistrust. Rybak glanced up and waved enthusiastically. Charlie went along with it because he was a good boy and did as he was told but did not smile. David waved back, only stopping when Rybak led Charlie off camera.

Prakesh snapped a pair of cuffs around the snivelling woman's wrists and led her away.

With no reason to keep watching, David returned to the soundproofed room. The old man was still making feeble suckling noises in anticipation of his sippy cup. Minotaur dangled beneath the gently clinking chains.

"He's safe," said David.

"I don't care."

"So why have you been watching him all this time?"

"Oh David." Minotaur's ruined face stretched into a pantomime expression of pity. "Are you really that naïve? It's not just me who's been watching him. Your son has become a star. He's very popular with a certain demographic."

David grabbed the killer's ears and squeezed them tight in his fists. Cord-like veins snaked across Minotaur's neck and temples. Despite the pain he managed something resembling a smile.

Seeing nothing but joy in the killer's eyes, David released his grip. He grabbed the sippy cup and helped the old man into a sitting position. The litany of feed-me noises grew ever more pathetic as the beaker drew closer to his mouth.

Minotaur watched his stepfather's scabby lips pucker around the plastic spout. David tilted the cup, allowing Alan to slurp down the fatal mix. The old man seemed unfazed that his usual gruel had been swapped with soup and a cocktail of potent sedatives. Within minutes the beaker was sucked dry and the old man's eyelids were starting to droop. His head lolled into the crook of David's arm, but he continued to suckle dreamily.

"Five grand," said the killer.

"What?"

"I sold your boy to a paedophile for five thousand pounds. I paid off some debts. I bought food. It was gone in less than a week."

Each word felt like a spike being hammered into David's heart. He remained still for a few moments as he considered his next move. Then, leaving the old man to drift away, David picked up the hatchet and advanced on Minotaur.

"You know," said the killer, "I watched it once. For a big man, he was very gentle."

CHAPTER SIXTY-SEVEN

When the story broke that David Knight was a mild-mannered author with no previous convictions, the news cycle went into meltdown. Tabloid headlines and column inches wrote themselves.

Christopher Wynn had sustained life-threatening injuries. If he ever woke from the coma, it would be to spend the rest of his days with severe brain damage. For many, this was a fitting punishment. For others, David had prevented justice from being served. An assessment as to whether the killer was insane – and therefore unfit to stand trial – could no longer be made. Depending on the publication, David was either a hero, or a dangerous vigilante.

Either way, the police were vilified for their incompetence. As for the detectives responsible for rescuing young Charlie Knight, they were consigned to a footnote. But while there remained many unanswered questions, and blame to apportion, there was something upon which everyone agreed – Jamie Hyde would be the sole recipient of the newspaper's reward. There was something pleasingly ironic about this vulnerable young man playing such a vital role.

Frank, meanwhile, received some unexpected news from Rybak. The detective informed him that the assault charges had been dropped without explanation. She could only speculate that it was due to Frank's association with the man who stopped Minotaur – or possibly the embarrassment of being bested by a pensioner.

———

Doctor Astrid Linderman's office was decorated in primary colours and furnished with matching chairs. Her medical diplomas were lost amongst framed pencil drawings of much-loved Disney characters.

Frank made unconvincing broom-broom and nee-naa noises while pushing a fire truck across a play mat. "Come on, Charlie, what about this one?" He cast a hopeful glance at the boy, but Charlie continued to stare at the floor. Plucking a spaceship from the toy box, Frank mimed a dramatic blast-off. "Wow! Look at it go."

Doctor Astrid sat cross-legged on one of several large bean bags. Slim and in her late thirties, she had a soothing voice with just the hint of a Scandinavian accent. "Charlie? Would you like to do some drawing now?"

The boy nodded but avoided eye contact.

She found him a large sketch pad and a selection of coloured pens, before leading Frank into the corridor. "I think I can help."

"I hope so. He's been bounced around from one doctor to another. He needs stability."

"I agree. And he hasn't said a word since it happened?"

Frank shook his head. "I tell him every day, how much he's loved, that he's safe, and that none of it was his fault. I just can't get through to him."

"In time we may see some of these barriers come down. But

we must be patient and prepare ourselves for setbacks along the way. There are no shortcuts."

Frank and Charlie strolled hand in hand along the high street. "What do you fancy for lunch?"

The boy shrugged.

"I know. How about a big plate of waffles and ice cream?"

There was only one place to go in Carlton Bridge for such a delicacy and that was Dickie's Diner. They were strictly off the menu for Frank, but he would enjoy watching his grandson tuck in.

As they settled into a booth, Frank spotted DI Rybak at a nearby table. She put down what was left of her bacon roll, wiped her mouth with a serviette and walked over to them. "Hello Frank. Hello Char–"

Before she could finish, the boy scrambled over his grandfather's lap and threw himself into Rybak's arms.

"Well, this is a nice surprise."

Frank smiled, clearly moved by his grandson's reaction. "Hello, Detective Inspector."

"Call me Maureen."

"Maureen... would you like to join us?"

The detective accepted the invitation, wrangling herself into a sitting position even with Charlie clamped around her. Conversation was polite but awkward. There were just too many things they could not discuss in front of the boy.

And so, instead of talking about David's trial, or the hunt for Peter Vaughan, they chatted about something of real importance – waffles and ice cream. Words like 'yummy' and 'scrummy' were used. And while Charlie remained silent throughout, at least he was smiling.

CHAPTER SIXTY-EIGHT

Frank's bungalow had been decorated and refurbished, transforming cold and dingy into warm and welcoming. The collage on the living-room wall was gone. The maps, Post-its and clippings had been consigned to the bonfire. The shelves, books, and family pictures were back where they belonged.

After Charlie's bath they sat on the sofa watching *Toy Story* until the boy fell asleep. Frank scooped up his grandson and carried him to bed.

Shortly after 9pm there was a knock at the front door. Immediately suspicious, Frank equipped himself with a screwdriver, and peered through the spyhole. Natasha Grand stood outside. Her slim face artificially swollen by the fisheye lens.

Pocketing the makeshift weapon, Frank opened the door. "Oh," he said, feigning surprise. "Natasha..."

"Hello Frank. May I come in?"

"Yes. Of course."

He showed her into the living room, and she settled into an armchair. "You look good, Frank. Really good."

"I had a bit of a health scare a while back. Since then, I've been doing as I'm told. Diet. Exercise. All that stuff."

"It's obviously working. I'm pleased for you."

"Is this to do with your father? Is he all right?"

"He's a fighter."

"He's one of the toughest bastards I've ever known." Frank watched as she struggled with some internal burden. "Natasha, why are you here?"

"I want to make amends. You came to me for help, and I turned you away."

"You didn't turn me away. Things have changed. I understand."

"I lied."

Frank's brow furrowed as her revelation sank in.

"I did what I thought was best to protect the company, my dad, and me." She averted her eyes, overcome by shame. "The truth is, there are still a few areas of the business that aren't exactly... let's just say... whiter than white. I could have helped you, but I didn't, and for that I'm sorry."

"Apology accepted." Frank's voice carried no trace of emotion. "Is that all?"

"No. Like I said, I want to make amends."

"I don't need anything."

"I'm glad to hear that, but I wasn't thinking of you."

CHAPTER SIXTY-NINE

"Turn around and put your hands behind your back."

David did as the prison officer instructed. He faced the cell's concrete wall as handcuffs clicked around his wrists.

Despite grand statements from the Home Secretary promising grass roots reform, change was yet to be seen at HM Prison Belkinwood. Inmates awaiting sentence were kept in a separate unit from convicted murderers, terrorists, and perverts over in the larger wings. Nevertheless, conditions were crowded and unsanitary. For many, the daily routine was tainted by the ever-present threat of aggression and violence.

It was recreation time. Inmates congregated along the wing in their own ethnic or gang-affiliated groups. Some played poker for cigarettes, chocolate, and phone cards. Others spoke in conspiratorial whispers or browsed through well-thumbed porn mags. A few loners, and obvious victims kept to themselves, loitering on the sidelines.

A man with a Celtic cross tattooed on his neck spotted David and began to clap. The reaction was quick to spread. Irrespective of race or creed, or position within the prison hierarchy, everyone joined in until it became a thunderous applause.

As David approached a door in the far wall it was unlocked and opened by another prison officer. The guards exchanged a curt nod as responsibility for their high-profile inmate passed from one to the other.

Ten minutes and another three heavy doors later, David boarded a security van. The handcuffs were removed, and he was locked into a steel compartment barely larger than a chemical toilet. A small square of opaque glass offered a hint of daylight but no clear view of the world outside. All David could do was settle in and make himself as comfortable as his claustrophobic surroundings allowed.

A crowd had gathered outside the courthouse, nearly all of whom were there to cheer for David. Homemade placards bearing messages such as *'You are a hero'*, *'Free David Knight'* and *'Justice for DK!'* were held aloft.

Uniformed police officers and court officials formed a cordon around him as the man of the moment was escorted from the van. He was back in handcuffs and flanked by a pair of no-nonsense prison officers. Reporters, camera crews and paparazzi closed in on them like a pack of ravenous wolves.

David kept his head down as microphones were jabbed in his direction. Cameras with long lenses bobbed over heads and shoulders. Shutters clicked and flashbulbs popped. As he was ushered into the building through its double doors, he heard one voice call to him above all the others.

I love you.

David looked back, straining to see past the entourage of uniformed police and court-appointed minders. Flashes strobed his view, but for a second, he caught a glimpse of Zoe, smiling that beautiful smile of hers.

I love you too.

The prosecution and defence had spent two weeks presenting evidence and cross-examining witnesses, taking turns to discredit, and cast doubt. David's barrister, the debonair and erudite Hugo Stokes-Devere, made an impassioned plea for leniency during his closing argument. He was matched, pound for pound, by his equally eloquent counterpart.

Throughout the trial, David had watched this pair of legal titans, in their black gowns and horsehair perukes, with a sense of detachment. He was under no illusion that a custodial sentence was inevitable. It was just a question of how long he would serve at His Majesty's pleasure.

The judge was known for her commitment to the letter, rather than the spirit, of the law. Her views on vigilantism were well documented. According to David's solicitor anything less than double figures would be considered a win. The very idea was laughable. Whether David was locked away in prison or walking around, free as a bird, Minotaur's last words would haunt him.

For a big man, he was very gentle.

Until Peter Vaughan answered for his crimes, David Knight would not rest.

"Have you reached decisions upon which you are all agreed?" asked the court clerk.

"Yes," replied the jury foreman.

"And what is your verdict on the first charge?"

Rybak's semi-regular visits to the hospital were not motivated by empathy, or pity. She had sworn an oath to uphold the law, but she had no problem seeing the monster laid out in such a pitiful state.

It had taken one of Europe's leading plastic surgeons to rebuild Christopher Wynn's face. Fillers and skin grafts gave the semblance of a nose, cheeks, and brow but even when it was fully healed, his visage would always be a blotchy meat mask. Wynn would never again assume the Minotaur persona. Nor would he walk, talk, feed, or wash himself. He was oblivious to the monotonous huff and whirr of the machines around him, and the comings and goings of hospital staff.

Rybak's phone chimed, notifying her of a breaking news story. This was followed by a flurry of text messages, no doubt related to the verdict in David Knight's trial. In bringing down the killer, he had succeeded where she and the taskforce had failed. But to what end? The premeditated nature of the crime, the horrific injuries he had inflicted, and Knight's lack of remorse all but guaranteed him a lengthy prison sentence. She could not help but feel responsible.

Frank switched off the news bulletin as Charlie padded into the living room. His grandson wore a colourful onesie and clutched his favourite Buzz Lightyear toy.

"Hello Charlie," said Frank, keeping a level tone. Although far from unexpected, the verdict was the worst possible result.

"When is Daddy coming home?"

These were the first words the boy had spoken since the rescue. His little voice had changed in a way that brought a lump to Frank's throat, and tears to his eyes.

CHAPTER SEVENTY

David was en route to Kane Hill, the Category A prison where he was to serve his sentence. By the time David was released, Charlie would be in his late teens. The stark realisation left David choking back tears. He knew this constant emotional struggle could not be sustained. His time on remand had been trouble-free but how long would that last when the Minotaur murders faded from the daily news cycle? To survive so many years of incarceration, David would have to keep such feelings buried deep.

His mind was filled with these bleak thoughts when the van lurched to a halt. David jolted forward, knocking his forehead against the metal door. Then came the sound of raised voices. At least two men were yelling. The rear doors clanked open, followed by more voices, thudding footfalls, and jangling keys.

"Hurry up!"

"I'm trying."

"Try harder!"

"All right! Don't shoot!"

The door to David's compartment swung open to reveal the terrified face of a guard. A second figure, wearing a nylon skull mask, held a semi-automatic to the man's head. "Get the cuffs off him, now!"

The guard was all fingers and thumbs as he scrambled to isolate a single key amongst a bunch of so many others.

David pulled tight against his restraints. "What is this? What's going on?"

"Shut up!"

"But–"

"I said, shut up!"

The desperate guard made a cack-handed grab for the gun.

"No–!" yelled David, but it was too late.

The masked man acted on instinct, smashing the butt of the pistol down hard. The guard shrieked, clutching his face as he stumbled backwards.

"What the fuck's going on in there?" a second voice yelled.

"Give me a minute." The gunman scooped up the keys and tried one at random.

"We have to go!"

David watched as the key was pulled free and another slotted into position. "You're making a mistake. Do what he says! Go!"

"There's no mistake, pal."

"You don't understand–"

"Get out of there, now!" called the second voice.

"Bloody thing!" snapped the gunman, as another key failed to turn. He tried again, several times. Eventually there was a small click and the first set of shackles fell away. David's leg restraints followed, and he was free. The gunman grabbed David's arm and hauled him out of the vehicle.

They were on a stretch of road that passed through a wind farm. On either side – and as far as the eye could see – were dozens of tri-bladed turbines in an expanse of gently swaying wheat grass. A low beating whoosh filled the air as huge propellers turned in endless cycles.

The prison van was sandwiched between a pair of idling Land Rovers. Another two gunmen, both wearing skull masks, aimed shotguns at the driver and a second guard. The two men laid with their faces pressed against asphalt. Hands clamped behind their heads, with fingers interlocked.

David caught their fear-stricken expressions as he was bundled into the back of a Land Rover.

"Don't even think about moving." The largest of the masked men jabbed a stubby shotgun at the prone guards for emphasis. They did as they were told, frightened to do anything other than breathe as doors slammed, engines roared, and the vehicles sped away.

David was free, but for how long? And more to the point, why? The breakout had been staged at what must have been the most remote point of the journey. His saviours – if that was the right word – had told him nothing. David's disorientation was compounded when a coarse blanket that stank of wet dog was thrown over him.

Throughout his life David had been reliant on others to get him from A to B. Friends, family, public transport, and a small fortune spent on cabs. That trajectory had reached its natural conclusion – transported by anonymous thugs to some unknown destination. All he could do was fear the worst.

Did Minotaur have friends, or a legion of fanatics, with plans to dispense their own brand of harsh justice? Had David been rescued, only to end up facing a sadist with a bag of tools?

He could only wonder about the guard who was smashed in the face and would probably be scarred for life. As for his colleagues, one wrong move and they would have been executed on the spot. All because someone had a reason to keep David Knight out of prison.

When the Land Rover finally stopped, David was hauled out onto a country lane. The light was fading, with only a few turquoise streaks trailing across the magenta sky. Parked nearby was a black Mercedes. A burly gunman grabbed David and bundled him towards the waiting car.

"No! Wait!" he yelled, but no one was listening. Wrenching his arm away, he lashed out, somehow landing an awkward right hook. David looked as surprised as the man he had just hit, who raised his own, much bigger fist in retaliation.

"That's enough!"

Natasha Grand stepped from the Mercedes. She removed her stylish, wing-tip sunglasses and fixed David with a laser-beam stare. "Mr Knight, please rest assured, we mean you no harm."

"Who are you?"

"My name is Natasha. I'm a friend of Frank's." She handed David a folded sheet of paper. He opened it, eyes narrowing as he read the words. "What is this?"

"That, Mr Knight, is where you'll find the man who raped your son."

CHAPTER SEVENTY-ONE

The sun-bleached hamlet of Alberra clings to a hilltop in the Toledo province of Castilla La Mancha. A dusty track meanders past olive groves and crumbling, white-stone dwellings. There is a general store, a small tavern, a 16th century church and not much else. Like so many other areas of rural Spain, Alberra has been ravaged by depopulation.

Felipe was one of its fifty or so remaining residents. Eight years old, and small for his age. A Real Madrid shirt and faded shorts hung from his skinny frame. He sat on a stony outcrop in the lower foothills, poking at the dirt between his scuffed trainers with a stick. Raven-black hair framed his cherubic olive-skinned features.

Peter Vaughan drew on the last inch of a soggy roll-up as he watched the boy. Eager to get the clearest view possible, he made a fractional adjustment to the binoculars' focus wheel. His vantage point was the kitchen window of a dilapidated farmhouse, on the outskirts of Alberra. Air conditioning was a distant memory, so the big man had stripped to his underpants. A flimsy nylon shirt did nothing to hide his bulging stomach.

Since Vaughan's arrival, he had counted only five children

in the village. Three were in their early teens and already showing signs of puberty. A fourth had some form of mental deficiency, which left young Felipe. He was, however, off-limits. Vaughan dared not risk attracting suspicion within the tiny hilltop community, but that did not stop him fantasising. His pulse quickened and the cotton across his groin tightened at the thought of a flesh-on-flesh encounter.

Eventually Felipe grew bored and tossed the stick away. He mounted a dusty pushbike and pedalled back to his parents' house. Vaughan set aside the binoculars and collapsed on a moth-eaten couch. This pitiful existence was driving him insane. Cooped up in a squalid little sweat box, day after day. His only entertainment was a gym bag filled with video cassettes.

These tapes were his most prized possessions. A stash of child pornography that had, over the years, gained near-mythic status. Most collections in the format had been lost, seized, or destroyed but this batch had survived. Upon fleeing his holiday home on the Costa del Sol, they were among the first things to be packed.

Vaughan checked his watch. Luis was due to arrive in a little over an hour. Along with supplies, and news from the outside world, he would bring word of Vaughan's next move. Somewhere, Vaughan hoped, more luxurious than a derelict shack in Alberra.

CHAPTER SEVENTY-TWO

Charlie bit his lip, in deep concentration as the picture took shape. It was nothing like the big yellow lion he had drawn after the school trip to London Zoo. His king of the jungle had been brightly coloured and full of life. This image was dark and jagged. Three dog faces glared from the page. A large one in the middle, flanked by two smaller creatures on either side. They all had angry eyes and sharp teeth.

"Charlie?"

Charlie looked up from his sketch to see Frank standing in the bedroom doorway.

"Can I come in?"

The boy closed the drawing pad and shuffled along so his grandfather could sit on the bed.

"Remember when I told you it wouldn't be long before you saw Daddy again?"

Charlie watched his grandfather expectantly.

"Well, something's happened. Something that will make seeing Daddy again difficult."

"He doesn't love me anymore, does he?"

"Your daddy loves you so much. More than anything in the whole world. Don't you ever doubt that."

"So why doesn't he want to see me?"

"He does want to see you. He just can't. Not right now."

"Is he in trouble?"

"Yes, but it's not his fault. He's a good man."

Charlie's face crumpled into a mask of sadness.

Frank looped an arm around the boy's shoulders. "I've got you a present."

Charlie sniffed. "I don't want a present. I want my daddy."

"I know, but I think you'll like it." Frank reached into his pocket and pulled out a silver-grey flip-top-style phone. "This isn't just any phone. This is a special phone."

Charlie studied the chunky device from all angles. "Why is it special?"

"Because it will only ever receive one call."

"Then what happens?"

"You throw it away."

"That doesn't sound very special."

"Ah, but it is."

"Why?"

"Because, Charlie, that one call will be from your daddy."

CHAPTER SEVENTY-THREE

Since the escape, David had spent almost twenty-four hours concealed in the back of various vehicles. For what would be the penultimate stage of his journey, he was hiding again. This time, stretched out in the rear of an articulated lorry carrying office supplies to Europe. The secret compartment was barely larger than a coffin and although ventilated, reeked of engine oil.

After clearing customs at Folkestone, the lorry boarded Le Shuttle, the locomotive service carrying private and commercial vehicles through the Channel Tunnel to Calais. It was a journey that took thirty-five minutes but David had been cooped up in the stifling darkness for what seemed like a lifetime. He was drenched in sweat. His head pounding from the noise, fumes, and constant vibration.

Why are you doing this? asked Zoe.

"I have to." David's voice was a murmur, as if he were talking in his sleep.

You're not that person.

"I am now."

Look at me.

David found himself nose to nose with his wife. "I miss you so much."

I miss you too, darling. But killing this man won't change anything...

Her eyes lost focus as her voice faded away. Blood trickled from her hairline. Slowly at first but soon becoming a steady flow that consumed her features.

"Zoe...?"

I have to go now...

"Don't leave me!"

You don't need her, whispered Minotaur from the darkness. *You need me.*

"No! You're not here! You're not real!"

Maybe not, but neither was your pretty wife.

David lashed out but succeeded only in driving his fist into the riveted steel. As the pain in his knuckles flared, David pictured himself using the flaccid meat of Vaughan's severed penis to silence the paedophile's scream. Then he saw himself dragging a blade along the man's stomach. Flesh split apart to expose a compact jigsaw of glistening organs. Intestinal coils slipped free in a bloody avalanche. A soggy mess of unspooling bowels landed in a heap between Vaughan's feet.

"Stop!" screamed David into the oily darkness. "Make it stop!"

CHAPTER SEVENTY-FOUR

Ray Keaton's official job title was 'Logistics Manager'. He was a salaried employee for The Grand Haulage Company, with generous pension benefits and a healthcare package. His actual role strayed some way beyond supply chain co-ordination and end-to-end order fulfilment.

Back in the days when Eddie Grand was calling the shots, he had surrounded himself with thugs and bully boys. Men with low brows, thick necks, and broken noses. Men like Frank Crocker.

Natasha, by contrast, selected her most trusted fixers based on their ability to go unnoticed. Keaton was the perfect example. His trim build and average features belied a highly skilled combat veteran. Three tours in The Gulf, followed by five years as a private security contractor had furnished him with an impressive skillset. He was at the top of a short list of people who Natasha trusted implicitly.

Keaton had prepared the export documents himself, so passed through French border control with zero fuss. Keen to check on his passenger, he pulled into the nearest truck stop. The sprawling way station offered secure parking for up to three hundred lorries. Truck- and tank-washing facilities were available as well as refreshment and laundry services for road-weary drivers.

Alighting from the cab, Keaton hurried around to the rear of the forty foot long semi-trailer, cut the ring seal, released the locking system, and swung the heavy doors open. Clambering into the back, he squeezed past ergonomic chairs, and flat-packed desks.

Having co-ordinated the loading Keaton knew which ratchet straps to release, and which palette to clear. He flipped up a pair of recessed handles and wrenched open the stainless-steel floor panel. David was asleep – or had passed out – in the narrow crawl space. He lay in a nest of rumpled blankets and empty snack wrappers. Three of his six water bottles were filled with urine.

"Mr Knight? Time to wake up."

Eyes snapping open, David gasped for breath.

"Steady. Take it easy."

"Get me out of here!"

"I can't do that."

"I need air! I can't breathe!"

"Someone could see you. You'll have to stay in here until we cross the border."

"When will that be?"

"Sixteen hours. Give or take."

David's shoulders sagged, as if wilting at the thought of another lengthy period of confinement.

"Or I could take you somewhere else."

"No. We stick to the plan."

"There's no hard border between France and Spain so you can sit back here all the way. I'll get you a change of clothes and toiletries. Maybe something to read. Any preference?"

David shook his head.

Keaton handed David a burner phone. "A present from Natasha. Your boy has one too. You could give him a ring."

David turned the phone over in his hands, a dumbfounded expression on his face.

"I'll be back in twenty minutes. Just don't get any bright ideas about going for a stroll." Taking his passenger's silence as tacit agreement, he exited the trailer.

David was left in the near darkness. He tapped the phone's keypad. The screen lit up, casting a pale glow across David's haggard face. Accessing the contacts, he found a number stored against the name, Charlie. He wanted, more than anything, to speak to his son but now was not the time. He had to stay focused.

———

True to his word, Keaton was gone for less than twenty minutes. He returned with shopping bags bulging with supplies. Leaving David to freshen up with wet wipes and mouthwash, he locked the back doors and returned to the cab. As the lorry shifted into gear and manoeuvred out of the truck stop, David stripped out of the suit he had worn in court and changed into joggers and T-shirt.

Imagine if this was a dream. Wouldn't that be wild?

Minotaur was leaning against a stack of boxes.

Or could it be the next stage in your mental breakdown?

"I'm not listening! You're not real!"

I want to help.

"I don't need help from a fucking psychopath!"

Think about it. You couldn't kill me. Despite everything, you couldn't bring yourself to cross that line.

"I didn't kill you because I wanted you to suffer."

Stop lying to yourself. You don't have what it takes.

Leastways, not yet. But with my help, you'll slit that bastard's throat without blinking.

David scooped up his discarded garments and hurled them at the killer. The jacket, shirt, and trousers hit a pile of boxes and fell in a heap. Clawing his hair, David slid to the floor. Eyes shut, and hands clamped over his ears.

You can't get rid of me. We're in this together.

CHAPTER SEVENTY-FIVE

The television had a fourteen-inch screen and built-in video player. Vaughan loaded a VHS tape bearing the tattered remnants of a sticker. As the machine clunked and whined into life, he drew the curtains and sloshed brandy into a tumbler. A date in blocky white text appeared in the top-left corner of the screen – 17-08-89. The image blurred as the camera swung around to settle on a young girl's face. She had curly, straw-coloured hair and wide soulful eyes. The picture quality was grainy and sallow from age and use. Every few minutes it rolled or stretched diagonally before snapping back to a 4:3 ratio.

"What's your name, sweetheart?" The off-screen voice belonged to Peter Vaughan.

"I'm Shelley."

"That's a pretty name."

The image wobbled and blurred as the camera was lifted upwards and mounted on a tripod. When it settled, Vaughan ambled past the lens and sat next to the child. He was several stone lighter, and his shoulder-length hair considerably darker. "How old are you, Shelley?"

"I'm nine."

"Nine? So, you're a big girl. All grown up."

"I'm not grown up. I'm only little. You're silly."

"Yes," said Vaughan with a throaty chuckle. "You're right. I'm very silly, aren't I?" He raised his hand and caressed the girl's cheek.

Shelley pulled away. "Who are you?"

"I'm your Uncle Peter."

"I don't have an Uncle Peter. Where's my mummy?"

The word became a hollow drone as the image froze and began to flicker. "No," murmured Vaughan, a look of horror on his jowly face. He hurried to the television and jabbed the eject button, but nothing happened. Pushing his fingers into the slot he poked and prodded until the cassette finally emerged. He plucked it out, but with it came a trail of shiny brown tape, a portion of which remained snagged in the machine's inner workings. In that moment, Peter Vaughan was as close to crying as he had been for years.

CHAPTER SEVENTY-SIX

D avid had no way to track his journey. The burner phone lacked GPS and the trailer offered no view of the world outside. Almost three hours had passed since their last stop, shortly after crossing the border into Spain. From San Sebastián, in north-eastern Basque country, David estimated they had travelled approximately two hundred miles. Assuming that was broadly accurate they were halfway to Madrid. From the capital city, Alberra was no more than an hour's drive.

The trailer had become an oven in the Mediterranean climate. David lay sprawled out on one of the palettes, a sweaty wreck of a man. Taking intermittent gulps of water, he stared at the insulated ceiling until his eyes stung and his vision blurred.

Given all he had endured a psychotic break was, he supposed, inevitable. Glimpsing, and on occasion, speaking to his dead wife, had been a portent for the main event. This manifestation of Minotaur had attached itself to David's psyche like a parasite. Poisoning his inner monologue and draining his last reserves of energy. The phantom presence was raw and relentless. It made David's skin feel corrupted. Like an inflamed rash, or a recently picked scab.

The infection had, however, revealed an uncomfortable truth. David had tortured and bludgeoned Minotaur to within an inch of his life. He could have delivered the coup de grâce or simply walked away, leaving his victim to die of blood loss. Instead, he had called the emergency services and remained with his victim until they arrived.

Why? Because partway through unleashing his rage, around the time Minotaur's nose and cheekbones disintegrated, David fell to his knees and screamed until his throat was raw. He had looked at his hands – bloodied and numb – barely recognising them as his own. There was no sense of guilt, shame, or remorse, just the unshakeable knowledge that he could do no more. Sucking down the last mouthful of water he wondered if he would encounter the same barrier with Vaughan.

According to Keaton's contact, the paedophile had yet to leave his farmhouse bolthole. Supplies were delivered once a week by a courier named Luis, although timings varied considerably. As David contemplated how best to catch his target unaware, the bottle crunched inwards. Empty, but for a few last drops of fluid clinging to the misty plastic.

David had been in the back of the articulated vehicle long enough to know they had left the motorway. Their speed had dropped significantly, the thrum of other traffic could no longer be heard, and they were travelling along an incline. Eventually the lorry rolled to a stop.

CHAPTER SEVENTY-SEVEN

The scrubland buzzed with the sound of cicadas. In the hazy distance were construction sites abandoned at various stages of completion. David's eyes were still adjusting to the blazing sunlight. He tried shielding his face but within seconds felt the scorching heat prickle his arm.

Parked by the lorry's cab was a seven-seater Model X Tesla. Its driver was a stocky man in a gaudy shirt. He and Keaton shook hands and exchanged a few words in Spanish. The driver turned his attention to David, appraising the escapee's dishevelled appearance. "¿Es este el hombre que atrapó Minotauro?"

Keaton nodded. "Si. Es él."

The Spaniard's face lit up with a broad grin. He barrelled over and wrapped his arms around David in an enthusiastic bear hug, whilst clapping him on the back.

It seems you have a fan.

David's eyes shifted to the killer. He stood nearby, silhouetted against the sun. *Tell them I'm here. I dare you. Let's see what your new friends have to say about that.*

After another minute of excitable chatter and handshaking the Spanish man waved them goodbye. He boarded the lorry and drove away.

"Are you all right?"

David nodded wearily. "Just feeling the heat."

Keaton plucked a bottle of water from a cool box and tossed it to David. Twisting off the lid David took several long swallows before pouring the remainder over his face and neck.

Keaton pulled a handgun from an ankle holster. "Have you ever used one of these?"

David shook his head, eyes fixed on the weapon.

Keaton screwed a large Octane suppressor to the barrel before loading a magazine into the weapon's polymer grip. "This is a Glock 19 semi-automatic. It holds ten, nine-millimetre rounds and one in the chamber. Lightweight and compact. Easy to conceal but watch out for the kick." To emphasise his point, he took the empty bottle from David and placed it on the ground.

Taking a few steps back, he held the Glock in a sure-footed two-handed grip and fired. The gun bucked as it spat out an empty shell casing. The round punched a hole clean through the plastic, sending the bottle dancing away across the dirt. "The trigger pull requires five and a half pounds of pressure. That may not sound like much but trust me, it will feel a whole lot more when you're face to face with him. Aim for the body. Chest or gut. He'll go down like a sack of bricks."

He passed the gun to David. "Give it a go."

Mimicking his instructor's stance, David levelled the gun.

"Breathe normally and take your time."

Minotaur stepped in front of the Glock, spoiling David's aim. *Is this really what you want? After all that effort you put into torturing me. Your son's rapist gets a free pass, does he?*

Bang! Dead. End of story. That's good enough for you, is it? I'm disappointed. I thought you had more imagination.

Sweat trickled into David's eye. Blinking it away, he tried to wrestle back control of his thoughts.

He used your boy and left him traumatised. God knows how many other kids he's abused or killed. If anyone deserves to suffer, it's him.

David squeezed the trigger. His instructor grinned as the bottle was punched even further away. "Nice shot. Do you want another go?"

"No. I'm good."

"Any questions?"

"Just one. Can I have a knife?"

Within moments of settling into the Tesla's back seat, David was asleep. A combination of the vehicle's luxurious interior design, its silky-smooth autopilot, and the air conditioning. It was the best hour's rest David had enjoyed in a long time. He awoke, yawning and stretching but refreshed.

Keaton resumed manual control and slowed to an idling stop. He pointed to a tiny hamlet in the barren hillside up ahead. "There it is. Alberra. Your man's in the farmhouse just outside the village. If you need anything else... anything at all... tell me now."

"You've done enough. What happens next, that's on me."

Keaton keyed his number into the burner phone. "Call me when it's done, yes?"

David nodded, knowing that outcome was far from guaranteed. They parted ways, David watching the Tesla until it was a dot on the landscape.

So, what's the plan?

David screwed his eyes shut, another pointless attempt at blocking out the killer's voice. It would take years of therapy to prune away those insidious tendrils. Without Zoe's stabilising influence, David was left with no option. When he opened his eyes, they held a newfound darkness.

CHAPTER SEVENTY-EIGHT

Spaghetti hoops simmered in a pan. For the third day running, this was to be Vaughan's dinner. Hiding out in a sweltering hellhole like Alberra was bad enough without having to survive on such meagre rations. He spooned the lumpen mess onto a slice of half-cremated toast. The washing-up had not been done so his plate and cutlery were smeared with congealed sauce from the previous day. He sat at a wonky table and tucked into the paltry meal.

His anger at losing the VHS of Shelley as a child had been eclipsed by an even darker rage. There was still no sign of Luis, which sent Vaughan a message that was all too clear. He had become an afterthought. Or, even worse, a liability.

When he was done eating, the hulking paedophile rolled himself a cigarette, struck a match, and drew the glorious nicotine-infused smoke into his lungs. Given everything he had done for the group, and the profits he had generated, it was an obvious sleight. He poured himself a large brandy and knocked it back in one.

Was this it? The end of the road?

His spirits were lifted by a slow and deliberate knock. "Thank Christ for that." Scraping his chair back, he lumbered down the narrow hallway, and opened the front door. There was no sign of Luis, or anyone else for that matter.

Vaughan scanned his barren surroundings. A drystone wall, a field of parched dirt, and a bumpy track leading to Alberra. But then, glancing down, he saw it. On the porch step, just ahead of his podgy varicose-vein-studded feet, was a straight razor with a mother-of-pearl handle. Vaughan stooped to pick it up. Thumbing the tang, he levered open the blade.

"What the hell...?"

"Hello Peter," said a voice from behind.

Vaughan turned and recognised the shabby intruder immediately. Even while on the run, he could not have failed to see David Knight's face plastered across tabloids, magazines, and news bulletins.

The paedophile stalked forward, brandishing the razor. "I'll cut you. I swear to God, I'll cut you wide open!"

"That's not what it's for." David pulled the Glock from his waistband. "It's for you to castrate yourself."

"What?"

"I'm giving you a choice. Castrate yourself and I'll walk away. Or I kill you. Your balls for my son's innocence. It's a good deal."

"Are you fucking delusional?"

There was a muffled crack as the Glock fired a single shot. Vaughan looked down in horror at the ragged stump where the big toe of his left foot should have been. "I'll fucking kill you for that!"

"No, you won't. The days of you making threats, hurting people, and playing God are gone. So, what's it to be?"

Vaughan snorted up a clot of phlegm and spat at David.

There was another muffled crack followed by the dull crunch of Vaughan's kneecap exploding. He unleashed a high-pitched mewl and gaped at the mess of dripping blood and shattered cartilage. Losing balance, he dropped to the floor. The cut-throat razor fell from his hand and skittered across the stone tiles. David loomed over the cowering paedophile and took aim at his other knee.

"No! Wait... I can get you money. So much money."

"I don't want your money. I want your balls, or your life. It's up to you."

"Don't do this... I'm begging you..."

"It's not a nice feeling, is it? Alone. Scared. Forced to do something against your will."

"I'm sorry! What I did to your boy... it was wrong. I know that. I'm ill. I can't help myself. It's not my fault."

"Bullshit!"

"I never hurt him. I never hurt any of them. I love children. I love them so much."

David's finger tightened around the trigger. "You need to stop talking."

"All I've ever wanted to do is make them feel special."

David kicked the razor back over to him. "Do it."

Vaughan picked up the blade and stared, bleary-eyed, at the gleaming steel. "Please... There must be a—"

"Shut up, and cut."

Vaughan's face crumpled as chunky fingers tugged the fabric of his Y-fronts aside. His testicles and penis resembled a button mushroom perched on an aubergine. The razor trembled as it drew closer to his scrotum. "I can't..." He moaned and dropped the blade. "I can't do it. I won't! Shoot me. I don't give a shit. You can go to Hell."

"Shoot you?" said David, with a look of surprise. "Who said anything about shooting you?" He grabbed the brandy and upended the bottle, sloshing liquor across Vaughan's legs, torso, arms and head.

"Oh Jesus Christ! No! Don't–!"

David struck a match and watched its tip blaze into life. With a flick of his finger, he sent the flame on an arcing trajectory towards Vaughan. The paedophile's liquor-drenched hair ignited on contact, transforming into a shimmering nimbus of blue and orange. The shaggy mane fizzed and shrivelled, burning away in seconds.

Vaughan screamed, arms thrashing wildly as fire ravaged his scalp, face, neck and body. Lobster-red flesh became taut and shiny until it blistered and burned. He howled in agony as his skin sizzled. Searing away to reveal subcutaneous tissue, muscle, and sinew. The nylon shirt crinkled and liquified, fusing to his bloated torso like hot tar. Vaughan's screams trailed away to become a series of strained whimpers. Finally, he went quiet and lay still. With the smell of scorched meat in his nostrils, and fire still dancing in his eyes, David turned away from the smouldering corpse and left the farmhouse. Minotaur was waiting for him outside. A silhouette in the afternoon sun. Only there was something different about his stance. As David drew closer, he shielded his eyes from the sun but caught the terrified expression on the face of a wiry Spanish teenager. The newcomer pulled out an old service revolver which he clutched in a twitchy grip.

Kill him, hissed Minotaur. *Shoot him. Do it now!*

David drew the Glock and took aim. The gun felt good in his hand, as if it belonged there. The truth was, killing this young man would have been so easy. David could see himself squeezing the trigger and watching as his target toppled backwards. There would be no guilt or regret. It was just something that had to be done. That was who David had become. Glancing at Minotaur he tossed the gun aside. The killer shook his head in a gesture of disbelief.

A shot rang out across the hillside. For several seconds nothing happened. Then, as if a spell had been broken, the teenager fled to a van parked nearby. He slammed the door and revved the engine. Gears crunched as the vehicle sped away in a spiralling dirt cloud.

David looked down to see a crimson rose blossom across the lower portion of his shirt. There was no pain. Just an icy chill that was at odds with the relentless heat. He staggered from the farmhouse, every movement a monumental effort.

Unable to take another step, he sank to his knees and tugged the burner phone from his pocket. He flipped it open, but the keypad digits swam in and out of focus. On his third attempt, David called up the two saved numbers. He made his selection and waited for the call to be answered.

"Hello?" The little boy's voice was choked with emotion.

"Charlie?" said David, struggling to keep an even tone. "It's Daddy."

"Daddy! I've missed you so much."

"I've missed you too, little one. Are you all right?"

"Yes Daddy."

"Where are you?"

"Granddad took me to see Mummy."

"Did you take her some nice flowers?"

"Yes Daddy. White ones."

"Good choice. She likes white ones."

"Daddy? Are you coming home soon?"

David tried to answer but the words caught in his throat. He fought for breath and tried again. "I don't think so... I'm sorry."

"It's all right, Daddy. I love you."

"I love you too. So much... You're my little star... Always know that."

"Yes, Daddy."

"Good boy... I have to... go now."

"Bye-bye, Daddy."

As the line went dead, David gasped and collapsed. He lay on the scorched dirt, in a slowly widening pool of his own blood. His eyes closed and he felt Zoe give his hand a gentle squeeze.

THE END

ACKNOWLEDGEMENTS

Thanks to Bob Gage for inspiring the most unpleasant line of dialogue in this novel; Mike Burry for being in my corner; and everyone at Bloodhound Books. I'll also raise a glass in memory of Mo Hayder. Gone too soon but a true guiding light.

A NOTE FROM THE PUBLISHER

Thank you for reading this book. If you enjoyed it please do consider leaving a review on Amazon to help others find it too.

We hate typos. All of our books have been rigorously edited and proofread, but sometimes mistakes do slip through. If you have spotted a typo, please do let us know and we can get it amended within hours.

info@bloodhoundbooks.com